DANNY ORLIS

AND

LINDA'S STRUGGLE

DANNY ORLIS
AND
LINDA'S STRUGGLE

BERNARD PALMER

Danny Orlis and Linda's Struggle
© 2024 by Bernard Palmer
All rights reserved. First edition 1964.
Second edition 2024.

Cover image: Adobe Firefly
Character illustrations: John Ball
Editor: Charlene Miskimen

Aneko Press *Youth*
www.anekopress.com
Aneko Press, Life Sentence Publishing, and our logos are trademarks of
Life Sentence Publishing, Inc.
203 E. Birch Street
P.O. Box 652
Abbotsford, WI 54405

JUVENILE FICTION / Religious / Christian / Action & Adventure
Paperback ISBN: 979-8-88936-014-8
eBook ISBN: 979-8-88936-015-5
10 9 8 7 6 5 4 3 2 1
Available where books are sold

CONTENTS

CHAPTER 1

BACK TO SCHOOL

It was a warm September morning when school opened at Fairview, Minnesota. The beach at the lake had closed for the season, but the water was still warm and inviting and the fishermen were still working the deep water with their jigs and spinners. Later, when the frost would begin to chill the shallows, the big northerns and walleyes would move out of the holes to feed. But now they were sulking near the bottom and had to be coaxed to strike.

Still Jim Morgan looked enviously at a carload of fishermen who passed him and Linda Penner on their way to their first morning's classes. "I wish I was going with them," he said.

"Hmph!" Linda shrugged her shoulders. "Of all the stupid things to do, fishing is the most boring I've ever tried. I don't see how you find any fun in it."

Jim grinned at her. "I suppose you'd rather be cruising around with Jack Ross."

She stuck out her tongue at him. "You think you're smart, don't you?"

"I'm smart enough to know you haven't got any business going with that character. He's bad news, Linda."

She bristled angrily. "You're just talking that way because Jack happens to be a friend of mine, that's all. I suppose now you'll run to Danny and Kay and try to get them on me about Jack, too. That's just about the kind of a person you are."

Jim Morgan lowered his voice. "Listen, Linda. I haven't got anything against Jack Ross except that he's not the kind of a guy I like to see you go out with."

"And just what's wrong with him?" she demanded haughtily.

"He drives too fast, for one thing," Jim said. There was a brief hesitation. "And according to the guys who've double-dated with him he doesn't treat his dates with the respect he ought to."

Linda Penner crimsoned and anger flashed in her dark eyes. "Jim Morgan, I want you to know that Jack Ross has always treated me like a lady. We've never done anything on a date that we're ashamed of." Contempt curled her lips.

"You'll have a hard time getting me to believe that."

They walked on in silence for half a block or so. Jim Morgan was the first to speak.

"You know, Linda," he began, "now that everything

turned out all right I'm sort of glad we got lost up in Canada[1]and had to live with those Indians for a while."

She stared at him in amazement. "You're glad it happened?" she echoed. "You can't be serious! It was positively the most horrid experience I've ever had in my life."

Jim grinned. "I'll have to admit that it wasn't a lot of fun when it was going on. But I'm glad that we had to go through it. What I'm trying to say, I guess, is that I think it was good for all of us."

"You must be out of your mind."

For the space of a moment or so his frown deepened.

"I don't know whether I can explain to you just what I mean or not, but staying out there with that Indian family the way we had to did something to me.

She snorted disdainfully. "It did something for me, too. Something I'd just as soon forget."

"I mean it," Jim repeated. "I didn't realize it at the time, but I'd been growing old spiritually. I would sit through the sessions at camp, but they didn't mean what they should have meant to me. I got to the place where my mind would wander during the message and I found myself sitting there, practically waiting for them to get over."

"I know just what you mean," Linda Penner said. "They left me that way, too."

"I don't think I realized it at the time," he continued, "but I was drifting away from God. Then

---

1 *Danny Orlis and the Ordeal at Camp*

when we were lost in the forest and I'd broken my arm and everything, I began to see that I didn't have any choice. I had to turn back to God. There wasn't anyone else to help me."

A superior little smile twisted Linda's pouting mouth. "You're beginning to sound just like Danny and Kay, Jim. You don't miss a chance to preach at me, either."

He bit his lower lip savagely to control his temper. "I'm not preaching at you, Linda," he exploded. "I was just telling you something that happened to me. When we were out on that island, I began to see how far I had drifted away from God. But when I prayed, it seemed as though He was right there, holding my hand. I wasn't afraid anymore."

For the space of an instant or two a strange look gleamed in her eyes – a look that was almost wistful. Then she shrugged her shoulders indifferently.

"Well," she said, pushing the subject aside, "you can be glad that it happened if you want to, but I'm not. All I'm glad about is that we got out of it without any of us being hurt really bad or killed or something."

Jim Morgan started to speak, but somehow words seemed empty and meaningless.

* * *

Jim had been counting on going out for football that season. In fact, he had been planning on it ever since they had moved down to Fairview from Canada.

However, getting his arm broken the way he did during the summer ruined that for him. He had given up any thought of being able to help the team until the coach came to him and asked him to be assistant manager and help take care of the equipment.

"We've got a big squad this year, Jim," Coach Brown said, "and a new student manager. We really need someone like you to help look after things."

Jim's eyes lit up. "That'd be great. When can I start?"

"How does tonight sound to you?"

"Great! It couldn't be better."

* * *

In school that afternoon, Linda Penner saw Jack Ross for the first time since returning from Canada. She met him in the corridor quite unexpectedly. Her heart fluttered and she felt the color surge into her cheeks.

"Jack!" she exclaimed.

He came swaggering over to her, a wide grin splitting his weasel face. "Hi, Kitten," he said. "So you finally decided to come back. Where have you been all my life?"

She made a face at him impudently. "I'll have to tell you all about it some time."

"Sounds like quite a story," he bantered.

"It is, believe me."

His laughter taunted her. "And what could be so exciting about a Bible camp? What happened? Did you go and get yourself saved or something?"

"Nothing like that." She squirmed uncomfortably.

"You'd better not," he exclaimed. "If you did, we'd find some way to knock that religion stuff out of you."

She snickered. That was what she liked about Jack Ross. He was a blast! Her heart was singing again.

They walked along the corridor for a moment or two.

"I didn't know whether you were comin' back to me or not, Kitten," he said. "Thought maybe you'd gone up there and found yourself a little Indian. Figured maybe somebody had beat my time."

A shocked look came to her face. "Jack," she retorted petulantly, "I don't even like to hear you talk that way, even if I do know you're joking. You know that I promised to be your girlfriend. I wouldn't think of dating anyone else."

His eyes narrowed, and the corners of his mouth twitched. "You promised, all right. I know that. And I thought I could trust you. But I've been hearing a few things, Kitten. And from the way I get it, I figure I'd better do a little checking up."

Her cheeks flushed. "If Jim Morgan told you anything, Jack, it's a lie," she fumed. "He's just lying to get me in trouble with you. He wants to break us up and figures this is the best way to do it."

Jack Ross chuckled until his shoulders shook. "Guess I found out more than I thought I did," he exclaimed, "when I talked to that little sister of yours."

Linda's lower lip sagged. "Did Becky tell you anything about me?"

"Did she ever!" He laughed again. "I found out all about you and that red-haired guy you chased after. You used to go out birdwatching with him, didn't you?"

"If Becky told you anything, she just saw enough to get her imagination started," Linda countered. "She saw Gregg Adams and me together once and–and started making up things that weren't true. You can't believe what she told you, Jack." Desperation rose in her voice.

"You don't have to explain anything to me, Kitten. I know what happened." The smile faded from his face and his lips curled. "You just don't need to think that I've been sitting around all the time you've been gone, either. I've been having my fun, too, Linda Penner."

The bell rang, calling them to another class.

"I've got to run, Kitten," he said. "How about meeting me on the front steps after school? I've really got my car ready for speed for you, Kitten. Come along with me and I'll give you a ride you'll remember all your life."

She swallowed her fear and managed a crooked little smile. "That–that sounds wonderful."

Jack was waiting for her on the steps of the school that afternoon when classes were out for the day. She smiled and waved to him.

"You did wait for me after all," he said.

"I told you I would." They started down the steps together. "I could hardly study all afternoon just for thinking about going for a ride with you, Jack."

"I don't know whether to believe that or not," he chided. "I suppose that's part of the line you gave that red-headed friend of yours, too."

Hurt gleamed in the girl's eyes. "Jack, what am I going to have to say to you to get you to see that you've got the wrong idea about Gregg? He doesn't mean anything to me. He never has. He–he's just a friend."

The Ross boy laughed curtly. "I can just hear you saying, 'But Gregg, Jack doesn't mean anything to me. He's just a friend.'"

She flushed scarlet. "Jack Ross," she exclaimed petulantly, "you know better than that. You're just talking that way to try and make me feel bad."

"Now wait a minute." His voice raised. "I'm the one who ought to feel bad. You were the one who cheated on me this summer. When you were late a few minutes ago I began to get worried. I thought you had headed for Canada to see your red-headed playmate."

Pouting, Linda Penner looked away. "Don't tease me like that. You know th-th-that's not true. You know what you mean to me."

Bitterness curled his lower lip. "If I didn't know, I sure found out this summer." In front of his car he stopped. "Gregg might have been a real heartstopper, but I'll bet he doesn't have a car as sharp as mine is."

She wrinkled up her nose at him.

They got into the car together. He started the engine and slammed it into gear. Rubber squealed as they took off.

Linda Penner gasped.

Grinning, Jack glanced in her direction. "What's the matter, Kitten? Are you getting soft since you went north for the summer? Can't you take it?"

She swallowed the lump in her throat and forced a thin, transparent smile to her lips.

"It–it's all right," she said uncertainly. "In fact, it's great. But I–I haven't ridden in a car like this for quite a while. You sort of took my breath away."

He laughed exultantly. "Listen, Kitten, you *never* rode in a car like this before you got in this one, and you've never ridden in one since. There just isn't any other car like it anywhere. And that's the truth."

He careened around the corner and roared toward the highway. It was several minutes before he spoke to her again.

"Now, give it to me straight, Linda. Did your birdwatcher from Canada ever thrill you this way?"

A smile lifted the corners of her mouth. He saw it and began to bristle.

"Now, what's gotten into you?" he demanded irritably. "I don't see anything to laugh about. You seem to think it's one big joke."

"I can't help it." She paused momentarily. "Jack, I do think you're jealous."

"Jealous?" The word exploded from his lips. "What makes you think I'm jealous of you? All I've got to do is crook my finger and I can get any girl I want at school. Don't you ever forget it." He cursed under his breath. "If you don't think so, just try me and see."

She forced the smile away. "Now, Jack, don't be like that. I promised you I wouldn't date anyone but you, and I haven't, even though I did have plenty of chances. I didn't have a single date all the while I was gone."

"That's not the way I heard it."

She moved closer to him on the seat and laid her hand on his shoulder. "You make me feel so bad when you talk that way," she purred. "You make me think that you–you don't like me anymore."

His lips curled derisively. "It's bad enough having you date someone else when you promised me that we'd be together. But saying I'm jealous of you is something I won't stand for. One more crack like that and I'll show you whether I'm jealous or not."

Linda Penner's smile widened. She wouldn't be able to mention it to him, but Jack was jealous. He actually was!

CHAPTER 2

LINDA MAKES A
PLAY FOR TOM

The Fairview football team started the season very well. They won the first two games by lopsided scores and squeaked by the highly rated Oak City eleven by the margin of a field goal. Jim Morgan was enjoying his stint as assistant student manager immensely. He and Danny talked about it at the dinner table a number of times.

"It would be a lot more fun to be out there playing," Jim said, "but the way I look at it, I'm real lucky just to be with the team."

Danny Orlis nodded. "That's the way I see it, too, Jim. A guy ought to be willing to do what he can to help the team, even though it's just being assistant student manager."

Linda Penner snickered and Jim's head snapped up quickly.

"Now, what's eating you?"

"If I were a boy, I wouldn't be afraid to play football. I wouldn't have to take a job like being assistant student manager."

Jim snorted indignantly. "I'm not scared. It's just that my arm hasn't gotten strong enough for football yet. I can do almost everything else with it and the doctor says the more I exercise it, the better it will be. But he won't let me play football this season."

"Anyone can believe that who wants to," she announced archly.

Jim Morgan felt the color creep up his neck and stain his cheeks. "I notice that guy of yours doesn't play football, and he didn't break his arm this summer, either."

Linda's lips curled and she smirked derisively. "It just so happens that Jack Ross doesn't care much for football. So he doesn't go out for it. But he doesn't go around trying to make everyone believe that he's crazy about the game, either."

Jim did not reply.

* * *

The following night after football practice, Jim Morgan walked home from school with Boyd Patterson.

"We've got a real team this year, Boyd, I can tell you that much," he said. "That new guy, Tom Channing, is just what we needed."

His friend nodded. "He's a real speed merchant,

too. All we've got to do is open a little hole for him in the line and he's through it and away for a long gain."

They crossed the street and turned toward Danny's home.

"We've got a good chance of winning most of our games," Jim went on, "if everybody can just stay eligible." He glanced at Boyd. "By the way, how're your grades so far this year?"

"That's one thing nobody's got to worry about this year. I've learned my lesson. I'm really working over the old books. Started it the very first day of school. I'm not going to be checked off the football team because of my grades if I can help it."

They had been so busy talking, they hadn't noticed the girl until they met her on the corner.

"Hello, Boyd." Her voice was warm and friendly.

His eyes lighted. "Hi, Robin. I didn't expect to see you here."

"Mother had some errands uptown and I told her I'd do them for her."

She was not a beautiful girl as some judge beauty. Her nose had an impish tilt to it, and a handful of freckles were scattered carelessly across the bridge. But there was a sweet, wholesome attractiveness about her. Fire danced in her soft blue eyes and the smile seldom faded from her lips.

Boyd Patterson gave no indication that he intended to introduce Jim to her, but Robin Evans took care of the matter charmingly herself.

"You must be Jim Morgan," she said.

Jim grinned.

"Oh, haven't you met?" Boyd blushed his embarrassment. "Jim, this is Robin Evans."

"You stay with Danny and Kay Orlis, don't you?"

Boyd left Jim and went over to her. "I told you all about Jim, Robin." He turned back to his friend. "I was going home, but I think I'll go with Robin on her errands. That is, if she'd like to have me."

She laughed.

"Oh, I'd like to have you go with me," she said pleasantly. "I've got a double armload of packages to carry. I've been wondering how I was going to get them home."

Boyd glanced over his shoulder in Jim's direction. "So long," he said carelessly.

Jim Morgan stared at him.

"I'm glad to have met you, Jim. I've heard so much about you."

Boyd Patterson frowned. "We'd better hurry," he told her. "The stores are going to be closing in a few minutes."

Jim stood on the sidewalk watching them and shaking his head as Boyd and Robin walked off together.

"A fine friend he turned out to be," he said aloud.

* * *

Robin Evans was at Bible club the next night, and so was Tom Channing. Tom and his family had moved to town during the summer, but Jim had met him the first day back at school. In fact, almost everyone in high school knew Tom, especially after the Fairview eleven won their first game.

When Linda Penner spied Tom, she left her seat and went over to him quickly.

"Oh, Tom," she gushed, "I've been wanting and wanting to meet you, ever since I saw you in the game the other night."

She stepped closer to him. "I've just got to tell you that I thought the long run you made against Oak City was amazing." Her voice caught. "I've never seen anything like it."

Tom Channing blushed self-consciously. "I had a lot of help," he said. "If it hadn't been for the guys in the line opening up holes for me, I wouldn't have been able to do a thing."

"I knew you'd say something like that. I could tell just by looking at you that you're *so* modest. But you can't hide what you did in that game. The others in the backfield had a lot of help when they carried the ball, too, but I didn't see any good runs they made. Why, you practically won the game singlehandedly."

Tom ran a hand across his face to hide the grin. "I don't know that I would go so far as to say that."

"I would," she countered. "You should have heard the way the people in the stands were talking about you. Everyone around me made some remark. They said they'd never seen such running. And the news raved about you, too."

She smiled her winsomest. "No, sir, you can't fool me with your modesty, Tom. You're the new star of Fairview High."

Jim Morgan, who had been standing there listening, snorted indignantly and muttered under his breath, "Oh-oh. Here we go again."

Indignation flamed in Linda's eyes as she turned and glared at him. But before she could say anything, Danny Orlis called for order.

"It's eight o'clock," he said. "I think we'd just as well get started."

Linda made a little face at Jim and turned to the new football player. "There are two seats over here, Tom."

Blushing delicately, he went over and sat down beside her.

Bible study lasted a little longer than usual that evening and the guys on the football team had to scramble to get home before the training curfew.

Linda Penner followed Tom Channing out to the porch. "I'm so glad you came tonight, Tom. You know, you're the first real, live celebrity I've ever met."

His eyes widened. "Me, a celebrity?"

"Maybe you don't think so now, but you will know it by the time the season is over." She paused significantly. "Everyone is going to be writing about you. And when you get to playing for Minnesota U, people everywhere will know about you.

Tom stood up taller. "You're just saying that to be nice."

"No, I'm not," she protested firmly. "It's the truth. Why, one of the men sitting next to me said he thinks you're as good as most of the college backfield men already. And you're still in high school."

Tom looked down at his watch. "It's almost time for me to be in. I've got to scoot or the coach'll have my hide."

Starry-eyed, Linda Penner smiled up at him. "Goodbye." There was music in her voice that did not go unnoticed.

He waved to her. "See you."

When she came back into the house, Jim Morgan was waiting for her.

"For cryin' out loud, Linda!" he exploded, "what were you tryin' to do?"

She eyed him archly. "I don't have the slightest idea what you're talking about."

"Now don't give me that stuff. For a minute I thought you were going to sit on Tom Channing's lap or ask if you could walk him home."

"I imagine that's supposed to be some sort of a joke."

Jim grinned. "The joke's on you. I think you're a little late making a play for Tom. Robin Evans already caught him and has a 'no trespassing' sign hanging around his pretty little neck."

Linda colored deeply. "He–he doesn't go out with her."

"You just wait and see. The other day they were walking to school together and he was looking down at her like a sick cow." Jim wrinkled his nose distastefully. "I never saw anything so disgusting – until tonight."

Linda Penner shrugged her shoulders in an exaggerated gesture. "It doesn't make any difference to me. I'm not interested in Tom Channing anyway."

Outside Tom hurried to catch up with Robin Evans, who was walking home alone.

"Hi!"

Her smile was warm and friendly.

"Oh, hello."

"Some meeting, wasn't it?" He fell in beside her.

"This is your first time at Bible club, isn't it?"

Tom nodded. "We didn't have anything like this in our school in Minneapolis. This is great."

She eyed him quizzically.

"I think it helps us a lot in our Christian lives," he said. "And Danny and Kay Orlis make it all so practical."

They crossed the street and turned toward Robin's home.

"That's what I liked about it. Since I took a stand for Christ, I've been trying to live the way I should, but there are times when it sure gets hard to do. A guy needs help like we got tonight."

"Of course, Sunday school and church and youth group are important, too," she reminded him.

"Oh, sure."

As they stepped off the curb, he took her arm and left his hand there until she drew away slightly. Tom frowned but said nothing while they walked half a block or so.

Robin noted the time. "You're really going to have to hurry, Tom, or you can't make it home before the curfew."

"Have you seen me on the football field?" he bantered. "I'm fast. I can make it home from your place in two minutes flat."

"I wouldn't want to be the cause of your breaking training."

He glanced down at her. "Are you as worried about Boyd Patterson as you are worried about me?"

"Oh, of course," she answered simply.

His face fell. "I was afraid of that."

"I wouldn't want to be the cause of anyone on the team breaking training," she reminded him.

They neared her home.

"I'd sure like to go out with you once in a while, Robin, he ventured. "That is, if you're not dating anyone or anything."

She laughed. "I'm not."

Tom hesitated briefly. "It seems to me that I've seen Boyd Patterson hanging around your place an awful lot."

"Boyd's a good friend of mine," Robin answered. "And we've gone quite a few places together. But I don't believe in dating exclusively – at least for quite a few years."

Tom Channing grinned. "We'll see about that."

She gave no indication that she had heard what he said. On the porch she turned to face him. "Thank you for walking home with me, Tom."

He stepped forward as though to put his arm around her. She retreated half a step and started to turn toward the door.

"Good night, Tom. It's been fun being with you."

"Can I see you again?"

"Maybe."

With that she slipped into the door and closed it behind her.

For two or three minutes Robin Evans stood in the hallway looking out into the darkness. Tom Channing was a lot of fun and he was easily the most popular guy in school. He was a Christian, too. Or at least he said he was. But there was something about him that bothered her. Something she had not been able to define. He treated her all right, but–

CHAPTER 3

WHAT'S WRONG WITH A LITTLE KISS?

When the Bible club kids had gone and Jim Morgan and Linda Penner were in bed, Danny and Kay went to their own bedroom.

"Danny, I was really encouraged tonight. I thought it was one of the best Bible studies we've had since we've been here in Fairview."

Danny Orlis picked up his Bible and held it lovingly with his calloused hand.

"I felt the very same way," he said, "even while we were studying. It wasn't that we had such a big crowd. For that matter, I believe we've had a number of meetings when the crowd was quite a lot bigger than we had tonight. But the kids really seemed serious. They were thinking."

"And they were willing to speak out," Kay added. "I got the impression they were all anxious to learn."

Danny opened his Bible and turned to a familiar passage in the book of Romans.

"If we can keep building on that foundation," Kay said, "we should see some results between now and spring."

Danny put the ribbon bookmarker in the Bible to keep his place while they talked. "I think I can tell you one thing about Bible club this year. Linda will be interested in coming for a little while. At least until she finds out if she can latch on to that football hero, Tom Channing."

Kay shook her head. "That was almost as disgusting as it was laughable. Tell me, Danny, did I ever act like that?"

He grinned at her impishly.

"Oh, sure you did. Most girls are a little boy crazy most of the time, and you were just like all the others. You chased me all the time."

Kay slipped off her shoe and good-naturedly tossed it at him.

Linda Penner had not gone to bed as Danny and Kay had thought when she went into her room and closed the door. Instead she was still standing before the mirror, slowly putting up her hair.

Tom Channing was cute. Cuter even than Gregg Adams or Jack Ross, for that matter. He had the cutest little smile and the broadest shoulders she had ever seen. Why, you could tell he was a football player just by looking at him.

And popular! Half the girls out at school would give a whole year's allowance just to have one date with him.

She breathed deeply, and for an instant, concern gleamed in her eyes. Robin Evans would have to start chasing after him.

Momentarily she laid the comb aside and studied her reflection in the mirror.

She shouldn't have any trouble getting him away from Robin. She was prettier than Robin for one thing, and her clothes were just as nice, or maybe even a little nicer.

And Tom Channing did like her a little bit. Anyone at Bible club could have seen that. That was another thing in her favor. And she did have a little head start.

She didn't care what anyone said. She was going to show Robin Evans whether she could get Tom away from her or not!

A slight, determined smile gleamed in her eyes. Thoughtfully Linda resumed putting up her hair.

Jack Ross would present a problem. When he found out, he'd roar until everyone in school would know about it. And the chances were he'd get so mad he would want to beat up someone.

And the girls at school. They'd all be so jealous of her when she started going with him that they'd just die. They'd positively die!

⋆ ⋆ ⋆

On Friday night there was another football game and again Tom Channing was the standout. He slammed a bullet pass into the arms of an end to set up the first touchdown and kicked a punt out of bounds on the one-yard line that put Crowell in a hole that cost them another six points. Linda yelled louder and got more excited than she ever had gotten at a game before, and when she got home afterward she was still bubbling with excitement.

"Jim," she said, "did you ever see such an interesting game? I'm so hoarse I don't think I'll be able to talk in the morning."

Jim Morgan laughed knowingly.

"I don't think that's going to do you any good, Linda. You'd just as well let your blood pressure simmer down. The way things look, Tom Channing's going to be tied up with Robin for a while."

Linda Penner made a face at him.

"It doesn't make the slightest difference to me who Tom Channing dates. He can go with all the girls in school for all I care."

Jim grinned at her crookedly. "I'll tell you what. I'll send Boyd Patterson over to see you. You can cry on each other's shoulders."

"Now, what do you mean by that?"

"He's carrying a torch for Robin Evans, the same as you are for Tom."

Anger flashed in her dark eyes. "Jim Morgan, you make me so mad I–I could just–I could just spit!"

She'd show him! She'd show him and Robin and the whole school who Tom Channing was going with.

They'd find out she could get any boy in high school if she wanted him bad enough.

When Sunday morning came, Linda got ready for Sunday school and church half an hour earlier than they usually went. She put on her prettiest dress, fixed her hair carefully, and came out into the living room, where she sat down, her purse on her arm and her Bible in her lap. She looked around the room uneasily. "Isn't anyone else going to Sunday school and church this morning?"

Danny Orlis frowned questioningly and glanced at his watch. "Sure, but it's still a little early. We've got half an hour before we have to leave."

Jim Morgan grinned at her. "How come you're ready so early all of a sudden? Every other Sunday it practically takes a stick of dynamite to blast you out of the house in time for church."

Linda straightened haughtily. "Really, Jim, you're unbearable." Contempt curled her petulant young lips. "I know you're juvenile and all that, but you don't have to show it so plainly."

"Juvenile" he snorted. "Who's juvenile? I just asked you a question, that's all. I suppose you think poor old Tom's going to be in church this morning, so you're all set to go after him."

"I don't have the slightest idea of what you are talking about." She stood and brushed an imaginary speck of lint from her dress. "I just decided to go to church early, that's all. You don't have to make a production out of it."

Jim snorted. "I suppose Robin Evans will be there early, too. She'll probably be waiting on the church steps for him."

Anger flecked the Penner girl's eyes. "You talk that way because you're jealous of Tom. You're jealous because the girls can't stand to be around you. That's your trouble."

"Hmph! The girls know better than to hang around me the way you're hanging around Tom. Somebody'd be apt to get clobbered."

"Well, you won't have to worry about it."

Danny and Kay and Becky were ready in a few minutes, and they all went to church. They didn't get there quite as early as Linda had hoped they would, and after Jim Morgan lipped off the way he did, she couldn't say anything about hurrying. But, as it turned out, they were early enough.

She took a seat near the back, where Tom Channing would be sure to see her as he came in, and waited.

Robin Evans was there, all right. Linda had known she would be, but she was sitting up front with a group of girls. Linda smiled inwardly. That was fine. In fact, it was just perfect.

When Tom came into the church foyer a few minutes later and looked around, she was carefully examining her bulletin as though she didn't know he was within blocks of her. She looked up, trying to act surprised when he came over and stood behind her.

"See," he told her. "I did come, just like I said I would."

She dimpled up at him. "Oh, hello. I didn't see you come in."

"You didn't think I'd be here this morning, did you?"

"I wouldn't have been surprised if you'd stayed at home to read all your wonderful press notices after the game you played on Friday night."

"I should say not," he answered. "Especially when there's a chance to sit beside you."

She moved over and he scooted into the seat beside her.

"So you liked the game," he said after a moment.

"Liked it?" she echoed. "It was marvelous. I don't think I've ever been so excited in my whole life."

Tom allowed himself a faint grin. "I didn't do so bad, at that."

Linda Penner glanced back in time to catch Jim Morgan scowling his disapproval and shaking his head. Deliberately she winked at him.

"How do you like living in Fairview?" she asked.

"I thought it was going to be terribly dull after Minneapolis, but now I think it's great."

A pout pulled teasingly at the corners of her mouth. "I suppose the change came when you met Robin Evans."

Tom Channing's eyes lighted. "She's cute," he admitted. "Y'know, I think maybe I could go for her."

"Now, I do feel bad."

"Don't let it get you all upset. To tell you the truth, I haven't decided whether I like blondes or brunettes the best."

Haughtily she straightened.

"If you plan on running some experiments in that direction, you can just forget about calling on me, Tom Channing. I'm not interested."

He laughed at her.

"Don't give up so easy. Who knows? The race may be over already."

Her smile was provocative. "I'm not so sure I'm interested at all," she told him. "I've sort of got a boyfriend."

"So I hear. But don't forget. I'll be around."

The Sunday school superintendent started toward the front. Tom leaned over to her. "How about sitting with me in church this morning?" he asked.

"I'd love to."

* * *

That night, however, Tom hung around after church and asked Robin if he could walk home with her.

She noted the time.

"It would be all right," Robin told him, "but we've got to go right home. I have a test first period tomorrow morning, so I've got to get to bed early."

"Suits me. I'm not supposed to be out late at night, myself."

He helped her into her coat, and they left the church together.

"The message tonight certainly was a challenge," Robin told him. "It made me see how important it is to have regular personal devotions."

He nodded. "I suppose that's right; that is, if a person has the time for it. To tell you the truth, I just don't find enough hours in the day for that, too."

"But we should. It's like the pastor said. Our personal devotions can keep us from drifting away from God and getting into sin."

"Sure, I know that. But a person's got to do something besides read his Bible and pray and go to church. We've got to live, too."

There was a brief silence.

"Last year our pastor challenged us to keep track of the amount of time we spent in that sort of thing just for a week. I thought I was doing pretty well until I actually saw it down on paper. I realized, then, that I was just giving God a little corner of my life."

Tom Channing did not answer her immediately, and when he did speak, he changed the subject abruptly. "I'm sorry we have to walk tonight. I tried to get my dad's car, but my parents had been invited out after church, or something, so it didn't work out."

"That's all right. This is such a beautiful evening, I think I'd actually rather walk."

"That's just the trouble." Disappointment thinly

edged his voice. "This is such a beautiful evening that it's too bad we have to waste it."

Robin Evans frowned.

"Now, just what did you mean by that?"

His grin was infectious.

"Nothing. Nothing at all." He stopped and looked up at the star-gilded sky. "Did you ever see such a pretty moon?" His tone was soft, caressing.

Robin laughed pleasantly. "My dad says it's just the same old moon," she answered. "If we miss looking at it one month, all we've got to do is wait and we can see it the next month."

He started forward once more.

"What a girl for romancing."

"I'm sorry, Tom. It is a beautiful night. I was just teasing."

"I suppose you've got some sort of an arrangement with Boyd Patterson."

"Boyd's a friend and the two of us have had some good fun together," she said frankly. "But we haven't had any sort of an arrangement or whatever you call it."

"I'm glad of that. I really like you. I like you a lot."

By this time they had reached her home and were standing on the porch.

"Well, good night, Tom."

He took half a step closer. "Is that all you've got to say?"

At first Robin didn't realize what he was driving at. "I don't think I follow you," she said curiously.

"That's no way to say good night when you really like someone," he told her. "You do it this way."

He bent down to kiss her, but she pushed him firmly away.

"No, Tom, please. I don't do that."

Indignantly he straightened. "Oh, come on, Robin: I know better than that. All the girls I've ever gone out with don't mind giving a guy a little good-night kiss."

"Not *all* of them."

"There's nothing wrong with a little kiss."

"I don't want to argue with you, Tom. We've had fun together. Let's not spoil it now."

"You're really going to be a wallflower," he said irritably. "That's all I can say."

CHAPTER 4

IS JACK JEALOUS?

Robin Evans went into her bedroom and closed the door, but it was a moment or two before she switched on the light.

Tom Channing was very nice. He was popular at school and a lot of fun to be with. And, he was a Christian, too. There didn't seem to be any doubt of that. He didn't smoke or drink and his conversation was clean and free of swearing. She had to admit that she couldn't help liking him. If he just would keep his hands to himself. She switched on the light and picked up her Bible to have her evening devotions before going to bed.

* * *

Linda Penner hadn't realized that Jack Ross would hear about Tom Channing sitting in church with her, but someone must have told him. Between classes Monday afternoon he came blustering up to her, eyes flashing, and with a surly set to his full lips.

"Hi, Jack."

He scowled at her but did not reply.

"I didn't know you had a class in this part of the building this period," she went on, her voice bright and cheery. "Or did you come over just to see me?"

"I came over to talk to you," he snarled. "I came to find out when you decided to go out for football?"

Linda studied him quizzically. For an instant she could not figure out what he was talking about.

"Just what do you mean by that?"

The corners of his mouth tightened angrily. "You know very well what I mean by that. From the way I get it, you're spending so much time at the football field after school that the coach thinks you're out for the team."

Linda Penner colored deeply.

"Jack Ross!" she snapped, "that's insulting. I won't even stand here and talk to you if you're going to talk to me like that."

"You're going to stand here and talk to me until I'm through with you. See? What's the big attraction? That's what I'd like to know."

"A lot of kids go out to watch the team practice," she said defensively.

"Sure, I know that. But you hardly even knew Fairview had a football team until you got acquainted with that moron, Tom Channing."

"That's not true, Jack, and you know it. I've always been interested in the team."

"I'll say you are. You're so interested now that you've even started to go to church with the guy. And don't try to deny that. I *know* it's the truth."

She shrugged her shoulders.

"Why should I? All I did was sit with Tom in church yesterday morning. There's no law against that."

He moved closer and stared hard at her.

"You're supposed to be my girlfriend," he snarled. "And here you're throwing yourself at this stupid Channing character. That's what burns me up."

Twin flames burned in Linda's cheeks. "I have not been throwing myself at Tom Channing or anyone else." She sucked in her breath sharply. "Who've you been talking to, Jim Morgan?"

"Don't you worry about who I've been talking to." His voice raised. "I've got my ways of finding out. And I found out how you hung onto him over at that stupid Bible club meeting the other night."

The Penner girl eyed him defiantly. "You're being ridiculous, Jack Ross," she informed him coldly. "And for your information I don't appreciate the fact that you had someone spy on me."

"I don't care whether you like it or not. You're my girl. I'm not going to have you running around with every guy in school who wears a football uniform. And you'd just as well know it right now."

Linda bristled.

"There are some things *you* had just as well know right now, Jack," she mimicked. "You don't own me just because we've gone out together a few times, and you're not going to dictate to me what I can do and what I can't."

Jack's voice raised, and several kids who were going down the corridor slowed to listen.

"We'll see about that."

Forcefully Linda controlled herself, but her eyes blazed and her little hands were clenched fiercely.

"You're making a lot out of nothing. Tom Channing is lonesome, and he and I have become friends. That's all there is to it and there's no reason for you to get so angry. I've felt sorry for him and tried to be nice to him, that's all."

"You've been nice to him, all right," Jack repeated. "But if you want to be with me, you've got to quit being nice to him as of right now. That's all I've got to say."

"If you're going to be so jealous of everybody I stop to talk with, maybe we shouldn't be dating anymore."

Anger whitened Jack's face. "All right, Linda, if that's the way you want it, go with your little football player. Make a fool of yourself running after him. But just remember this. You're not going to come crawling back to me when the season's over. You go out with him and I'm through with you. Understand? One more date with Tom Channing and it's the end of everything between you and me."

Linda's attractive young face flushed crimson.

"And what do you expect me to do?" she demanded hotly. "Cry about it?"

Jack Ross whirled on his heel and stormed away.

For a short space of time Linda Penner looked after Jack. Just as she had figured, he was mad. He was awful mad. He was so mad he wouldn't be back.

Her own temper seeped away.

She knew better. Jack would be back, all right. He was more interested in her now than he had ever been before.

A thin smile was playing on her lips as she walked slowly on to class. Here she had been worrying about whether she would have a boyfriend during school. Now, there were two fighting over her.

That wasn't bad. That wasn't bad at all.

* * *

Linda Penner's attendance at youth group had been careless and haphazard since she came to live with Danny and Kay Orlis. It had been a big waste of time as far as she was concerned, and she had found one excuse and then another for missing the meetings. When she thought she could get away with it, she had even gone somewhere else and pretended she had been to church. But now that Tom Channing was going, she attended.

Robin Evans was there, too, but the following week Linda contrived to sit next to Tom, and when the meeting was over, he asked to take her home. Her heart leaped, but she pretended to hesitate.

"I'd like to, Tom, but I'm not sure whether I should or not," she said. "I came with Jim Morgan. I really should go home with him."

"I know Jim. He's not going to care whether you go home with him or not."

"Maybe he won't," she answered. "But I don't know about Danny and Kay Orlis. They've got some weird ideas."

"If they give you trouble," he said, "I'll come over and have a heart-to-heart talk with them. A girl your age ought to be permitted to go out with a guy if she wants to."

He helped her into her coat.

Linda could scarcely believe it was true. Tom had come and sat beside her in church, but that had been casual. It might have happened with any girl. This was different. It was more like a real date. Her heart sang. What would Jack Ross and Robin Evans have to say now?

"We're really in luck," Tom said. "I've got Dad's car tonight."

"That's nice."

He eyed her narrowly. "You don't have to go right home, do you?"

There was a short hesitation. Not much. Just enough to let him know that she could get along without going with him if she had to.

"Danny and Kay will probably jump down my throat when we get in," she said, "but I'm used to that. They're after me about something or other most of the time."

He looked down at her, sympathy in his eyes. "They must really treat you rough. Aren't they Christians?"

"They talk as though they're just about the best Christians in the whole world," she complained, "but you ought to see what it's like around home when there's nobody else there. They act different then."

On the front steps Tom Channing paused and looked about. A frown crossed his handsome face.

"What's the matter?" Linda asked. "Did you forget where you parked the car?"

"There's Boyd Patterson and Robin Evans. What do you say we take them along?"

Linda smiled triumphantly.

"Let's. That sounds like fun!"

Boyd and Robin got into the back seat with them.

Tom turned and eyed Robin significantly. "Well," he said, "where do you want to go?"

Boyd turned to his companion. "How about it, Robin?" he asked. "Is there any place you especially want to go?"

"It doesn't make any difference to me."

Tom turned around again. "How about lovers' lane?" he asked.

Boyd acted as though he hadn't even heard him. "Why don't we ride around town for a little while and then go have a sandwich or something?"

"I'd rather go to lovers' lane. There are a lot of good places to park around there. Just ask me. I haven't been here very long, but I know them all."

He turned as though to head out of town.

"Tom," Boyd broke in quickly, "if you're going out somewhere to make out, you'd better let us out first."

The youthful driver was incredulous.

"What?"

"It's only a few blocks over to Robin's," the Patterson boy said. "You can let us out here."

Tom Channing snorted.

"Don't be an idiot."

Nevertheless, he turned at the next corner and they rode around. It wasn't long, however, until he dropped Boyd and his date off at Robin's house.

"Thank you, Boyd, for speaking out when Tom wanted to go somewhere to make out," Robin said.

Boyd smiled. "I don't think a Christian ought to get himself into a situation like that."

"I feel the same way as you do, and I was wondering what I was going to say when you took over for me."

They sat down on the steps together.

"You know, Robin," Boyd went on. "I can't figure Tom Channing out. He's a Christian. There's no doubting that. But he's sure got some funny standards."

"I don't want you to say anything to anyone else about this," Robin said, "but I found that out the other night. I had a good time with him, but he kept wanting to put his arm around me and kiss me. A lot of unsaved guys I used to go with treated me with more respect and consideration than he did."

Boyd nodded. "For some reason I've been thinking

a lot about that lately. It makes a guy a little sick to hear some of these Christian guys when they get together and start talking about their dates and what they do when they're out. You'd sure never know that they profess to be believers."

"And some Christian girls have got the idea they've got to let the guys maul over them if they're going to be popular," Robin added. "But if I've got to do that to be popular, I just don't want any dates."

Boyd looked at her. "We're not all like Tom Channing, Robin. I think you should know that. There are plenty of Christian guys who want to treat their dates with respect."

Her smile was warm and friendly.

"You've already shown me that, and I appreciate it – more than you'll ever know."

CHAPTER 5

THE DISTURBING BOOK

Tom Channing and Linda Penner let Boyd and Robin out of the car in front of the Evans home and drove slowly away. After two or three minutes Tom glanced in his date's direction.

"Where to now?" he asked.

"Anywhere." She laid her back on the seat and closed her eyes luxuriously. "It doesn't matter to me as long as you don't take me home right now."

Tom grinned appreciatively. "I'm sort of glad we dumped Boyd Patterson and Robin. They turned out to be pretty lame."

Linda straightened and faced him. "I don't know," she said defensively. "I've always thought Boyd Patterson was a real nice guy."

"That's just the trouble," he complained. "He's too nice."

There was a short silence.

"Let's not talk about Boyd and Robin, Tom. There's no use in spoiling a good evening."

"Suits me."

He put his arm about her and gently pulled her closer to him. "Come on over and be sociable."

Linda's shoulders stiffened and she sat forward slightly. He did not release his grasp on her shoulder.

"Don't, Tom," she said softly. "Please."

He snorted. "Now you sound just like Robin Evans. She tried to play that 'hard to get' stuff when she was out with me."

Linda was silent momentarily.

"What's the matter with you, Linda?" he demanded irritably. "Don't you like me?"

"Of course, I do. I–I like you a lot."

"Then what's the harm in showing it?"

She bit her lips to keep them from trembling.

"I–I do like you, Tom, and I enjoy being with you. But I–I just don't like to do things like this. It seems so-so cheap."

"It isn't cheap when you like a guy and he likes you," he told her. "I'll bet you don't keep Jack Ross a mile away from you."

"I–I–" The words drifted off into space.

Tom Channing pulled her head over to his shoulder.

"Don't act as though I'm poison or something. I like you. I want you to be my girlfriend."

Linda Penner cringed inwardly. She should make Tom take her straight home, but she couldn't do that.

After all, he was the most popular guy at school and all the other girls wanted to go out with him.

If she didn't let him do some of these things, he would probably never ask her to go out with him again, and she didn't want that. She'd just die if he tossed her over now. Besides, it was like Tom said. Everybody was doing it, so there couldn't be much wrong with it. She just hadn't had very many real dates. That was the trouble. Girls probably had to go along with a little making out if they were going to be popular at all.

Still, she was glad when he looked at his watch and turned toward the Orlis home.

"I've got to get you home and run, Linda," he said. "I'm going to be late now if I don't get a move on."

Nevertheless, on the porch he took time to kiss her twice and ask if he could see her again.

"I'd love it," she said breathlessly.

"Good. You'll be hearing from me."

Happily she pushed her hair back into place. Tom Channing wanted to go out with her again. Tom, the football star, wanted to go out with her instead of Robin Evans or anyone else in school. She tingled with excitement. Let Jack Ross storm about that if he wanted to.

Kay Orlis was standing near the door when Linda came in. The girl's eyes widened.

"Kay, are you still up?" she asked incredulously.

"I waited up for you."

The Penner girl sat down, petulantly, and eyed Kay. "Well, let's have it," she said scornfully. "Give me lecture 327 so I can go and get to bed."

"Linda, that is no way to talk to me. You are over an hour later than you told me you would be."

"I–I'm sorry, Kay," Linda said, "but Tom Channing and I got to talking as we rode around, and we just forgot what time it was. It won't happen again."

But Kay was not so easily placated.

"Linda, I've told you repeatedly that we want to trust you. But you've got to show us that you are worthy of being trusted first. You have a good watch; you could have kept watching it so you could get in on time." She paused momentarily. "You've just got to learn to be responsible."

There was a brief silence.

"I'm afraid I can't let you go out on any dates next week," Kay said.

The girl's face clouded petulantly, and she got quickly to her feet. "That's the way it's always been around here," she snorted. "You figure the very worst and start punishing me before I get a chance to explain anything."

Tearfully she fled to her room.

When Kay Orlis entered the kitchen several minutes later, Danny was sitting at the table reading a small booklet. He looked up.

"Well, I see Linda finally got home."

Kay pulled up a chair and sat down. "Yes, she came in just now. But, Danny, I'm very concerned for her."

"Are there any new developments that make the situation any worse than it has been?" he asked.

Kay nodded. "I was beginning to get worried when she was more than an hour late," she said, "so I went to the window to look out and see if she was in the car that had just driven up."

"Was something wrong?"

"I'm afraid so." Kay's forehead wrinkled. "She let the guy she was with kiss her good night, and when she came in, she was in very high spirits."

"I've been quite disturbed about the fact that she's still going out with Jack Ross," Danny said. "He isn't good for her. But there doesn't seem to be much we can do to keep her from dating him. If we forbid her to go out with him, I'm afraid she would just sneak out and date him behind our backs."

"I don't know whether she was telling me the truth or not, but she said she was with Tom Channing tonight."

"Come to think of it, Jim did say she had gone off in Tom's car from church."

Danny handed Kay the booklet he had been reading.

"Did you see this?"

She read the title aloud.

"*Dating Tips for Christian Teens.* That looks interesting."

"It is. And what's more, it's a very practical booklet. It's right down where these kids live."

Kay took it and read for a few moments.

"This is good, Danny," she said. "It's wonderful. In fact, it's just exactly what Linda needs – if we could just get her to read it."

"I don't think there's much question but that she'd read it," Danny replied. "Most girls her age are interested enough in dates and dating that they'll read anything they can find on the subject."

Kay turned the pages of the book and checked the chapter headings.

"This certainly covers about everything, doesn't it?"

"I'll say. And it's in simple, everyday language. It ought to be a lot of help for most kids."

"After taking a look at it, I agree with you, Danny," Kay said. "I'm sure Linda would read this if she had a copy. Just the headings are fascinating enough to make you want to get into the book."

Danny Orlis got up and poured himself a glass of milk while Kay continued to read.

"I've been thinking about the kids in Bible club, Kay. I think we ought to spend some time telling them about it the next time we get together. It's the sort of thing that ought to be in the hands of every one of our kids."

"It would be wonderful for them," Kay agreed, "but do you suppose their parents would object?"

"I don't know why."

"It's all in very good taste, but the thought occurred to me that some parents might not want these things brought up to their girls."

Danny thought for a moment or two. "I suppose some of them might have objections," he said, "but this deals with a subject that is so serious we've got to do what we know is right. This is a wicked world we're living in. Unless we warn our Christian kids of what they're facing, unless we point out the dangers and pitfalls so they can avoid them, we're really not doing our job. And if serious trouble comes because we don't have courage enough to follow the leading of the Lord, we're at fault."

"This booklet would have been a big help to me when I was Linda Penner's age," Kay said.

"I would have gotten a lot of help out of it, too," Danny told her.

* * *

Linda Penner had not even thought about the fall all-school party until the announcement was put out two or three days after Tom Channing took her home from youth group. Now that was one thing Tom could take her to.

Excitement tingled through her body. All she had to do was work out a plan and get to talking to him before he got a date with someone else. That very afternoon she contrived to see him and talk about the party.

"I don't know, Linda," he said indifferently. "I guess I knew there was a party sometime soon, but I don't know whether I'll go or not. I haven't decided yet.

"Oh, you can't stay home from that party," she told him. "It's going to be lots of fun. Everybody in school will be there."

"The football season is still on, and I've got to stay in shape. I don't like to be out so late."

Her eyes narrowed and a frown marred her pretty face. "That didn't bother you the other night."

Fear glittered in his eyes. "Don't say that out loud," he whispered. "Somebody might hear you, and then I would be in trouble."

"Oh, they couldn't do anything to you regardless of what time you get in," she told him. "You're the star. They wouldn't have a chance of winning without you."

"You just don't know the coach if you think he wouldn't dare do anything to me. He'd kick me off the team just as quick as he would anyone else. So just keep quiet about the other night, will you?"

"You don't have to worry. I'm not going to tell anyone how late you got in." Her laughter was fun and taunting. "Right now I'm more interested in the all-school party. You wouldn't have to stay until it was over if you didn't want to," she said. "You could go home almost any time you'd want to. I'd understand." She caught herself and blushed furiously. "I mean, everybody would understand why you had to leave."

He pushed his fingers through his shock of dark hair, "I don't know whether I'm interested in going to the party or not," he hedged. "I'll have to think it over."

Her temper surged. What would Jack Ross say if Tom didn't take her to the party and she had to go alone? She could hear him now. He would never quit taunting her about it. And what about the other kids who expected her to have a date with Tom?

She just wouldn't go. That was all there was to it. If Tom didn't take her, she'd get a bad headache or something and stay at home.

Linda carefully avoided mentioning the party to anyone, and it was not until the day before it was to be held that anyone asked her if she was going.

And then it would have to be Jim Morgan. He came home that evening shortly after six o'clock and accosted her.

"Well, Linda," he said knowingly, "are you all set to go to the big party tomorrow night?"

She acted as though she had not even heard him.

"You've really got me guessing about tomorrow night, Linda," he continued. "How are you going to manage it with two boyfriends? Are you going to have Jack Ross on one side and Tom Channing on the other?"

Her lips curled bitterly.

"I shouldn't even bother to answer you, Jim, but for your information, I don't even think I'm going."

He laughed. "Oh, come now. Don't give me that. You'll be there, all right. You wouldn't stay away from a party – any kind of a party. Especially when you've got two boyfriends. The thing that has got me curious is how you're going to manage with two of them fighting for you. Is there going to be a real battle or have you fed them tranquilizers?"

Crimson stained Linda Penner's cheeks, but her voice was edged with indignation. "Really, Jim," she told him, "you're so juvenile I'm not even going to answer you."

"This is one party I'm not going to miss," he snickered. "I'm going to be right on the front row."

Linda wrinkled her nose at him.

CHAPTER 6

THE ALL-SCHOOL PARTY

Linda Penner had been hoping desperately that Tom Channing would say something more to her about taking her to the all-school party. But he did not, although she gave him plenty of opportunities. He had said he didn't think he was interested in going, but that certainly didn't seem likely. He acted as though he was always ready for a good time. It could be that he was just pretending not to be interested so he could take Robin Evans. He spent plenty of time watching Robin whenever she was around.

The thought stabbed deeply into Linda's heart.

If that was the way it was, Tom didn't need to think that she was going to sit around and wait for him to come and ask her or take a chance on having to sit at home. She'd show him. She'd find someone else to take her to the party.

That afternoon she made a point of stopping Jack

Ross in the hall and talking with him. A provocative little smile toyed with the corners of her mouth.

"Oh, hello, Jack," she said. "It's so good to see you."

His eyes were hostile and his manner sullen and uncommunicative.

"I'll bet."

"Honestly, it is. It's been so long since you and I have had a chance to talk."

"What's the matter?" he demanded. "Are you getting tired of football?"

The color came up into Linda's face, but she pretended to ignore it.

"Jack," she said, "please don't talk that way. I don't want to start arguing with you again."

"Don't blame me for the arguments," he retorted. "I'm not the one who started them."

She completely ignored his angered remark.

"I've been thinking about you and the party tonight all afternoon." Her eyelids lowered. "Are you going?" she asked softly.

His laughter was hollow and mirthless. "You didn't think that I was going to sit at home and mope just because I'm not going out with you anymore, now did you, Linda?" he demanded. "I told you I was going to find me a girl who appreciates me. That's just what I've done."

Her face clouded, and for a brief moment her lips trembled uncertainly. "Is–is it anyone I know?"

"Maybe you know her," he said curtly, "and maybe you don't. You'll just have to wait until tonight to find out."

Her young body stiffened, and anger flashed indignantly in her eyes. "I don't think I'll bother. It doesn't concern me in the least who you take to the party, Jack Ross. You can take a dozen girls, for all I care. I was just asking to be friendly and–and to show that I–I don't care who you date. So there."

Linda Penner hurried off before he could read the hurt that rushed to her eyes.

She was late getting home from school that afternoon. She fooled around uptown and stopped in the shop for a lime drink before going home. When she finally got back to the Orlis home, she got out her books and began to study, trying hard to forget the party.

Sometime later, Kay Orlis came home and found her sitting alone in the living room. "Hadn't you better hurry, Linda?" she asked.

The girl's face paled slightly. "What for?"

"Isn't this the night of the big school party that you and Jim have been talking about?"

She shrugged her shoulders indifferently. "Oh, that," she retorted. "I'm not going."

Kay's face registered her surprise. "Not going? But I thought you were the one who was so excited about it when you saw the announcement out at school last week."

Linda Penner tried hard to act as though it didn't matter to her at all. "I was interested in going," she began, "until I found out that it was going to be a dance." She paused, eyeing Kay carefully to gauge the effect of her words. "When the kids told me that, I decided it was no place for me, so I'm not going."

Kay Orlis eyed her strangely, but questioned her no further.

Shortly after dinner that evening, Linda announced that she was going into her bedroom to study. That was the last anyone saw of her until morning.

At breakfast Jim Morgan squinted across the table at her. "What happened to you last night, Linda?" he wanted to know.

She glanced at him cautiously. "What do you mean?"

"I looked all over for you at the party," he said, "but I didn't see you. What happened? Were you afraid your boyfriends would have a duel over you or something?"

Her face went ashen, but she drew herself up to her full height self-righteously.

"You're such a good Christian, I'm surprised that you were even there, Jim. I didn't think you would go to a dance."

"Dance?" he echoed. "It wasn't a dance. It was just a real cool party. It's prob'ly the only party we'll have all year that isn't a dance. You should've been there."

Linda Penner flushed. "They–they told me it was going to be a dance," she said lamely. "That's all I know."

"Somebody told you wrong," Jim retorted. "We played a lot of games and had lots of food. It was great."

Linda then looked up at Kay defensively. "I was told it was going to be a dance, Kay," she said uncertainly. "That's honestly what I thought it was going to be.

If–if I'd known it was just going to be an ordinary party, I'd have been there."

A teasing little grin impishly lighted Jim Morgan's face. "Maybe it was a good thing you didn't go," he said. "Your old boyfriend was there, Linda. You prob'ly would have had your poor little heart broken right in two if you could have seen him."

Linda shrugged her shoulders and hoped, desperately, that no one knew how much she cared.

"If you think it bothers me that Jack Ross had a date last night you've got to think again. I'm not the least bit interested in Jack Ross or who he was with. That doesn't mean anything at all to me."

Danny came in just then. "Hi, kids," he said. "I'm glad you're still here. I want to talk to both of you." He pulled up a chair and sat down. "Think we'll have a good crowd out for Bible club tonight?"

Jim Morgan looked up. "I don't know why we shouldn't," he said. "The kids sure enjoyed the last meeting. They were talking about it around school for a couple of days."

"I'm glad to hear that, Jim. I thought maybe the party last night would keep some of them away."

Jim Morgan shook his head. "It shouldn't keep anybody away, Danny. We got out early. I was home by ten-thirty." He glanced quickly in Linda's direction. "Of course, I don't know what time Jack Ross got home. He had a date to the party and – wow!"

She made a face at him.

"I'd sure appreciate it if you'd both talk up Bible club all you can," Danny said. "We're going to have something special, and I'd like to have a good crowd out for it."

Interest kindled in the boy's eyes. "What is it?"

"Oh, no, you don't," Danny countered. "You're going to have to wait until tonight to find out, just like the rest." He turned to Linda Penner. "You'll help spread the word, too, won't you, Linda?"

"I suppose so." Her frown deepened. "But I don't think it'll do any good. Nobody wants to come to that stupid Bible club, anyway."

She pushed back from the breakfast table and stood slowly.

Linda Penner didn't invite anyone to Bible club that night. She didn't intend to, even when she told Danny that she would. But Jim did a good job of spreading the news. By eight o'clock, when Danny Orlis got up to speak, the living room was packed.

"It's good to see all of you here tonight," he said. "As you may already know, we've got something very special for you."

He took the booklet *Dating Tips for Christian Teens* from his pocket and held it in his hand for all to see.

"We're going to have our regular Bible study tonight, but not until after I talk with you for a few minutes."

The kids leaned forward expectantly.

"I want to tell you about this booklet Kay and I got this week. It is one that is important to all of you. I think each one of you should have a copy."

He paused and the eyes of the kids fastened on him.

"This isn't just an ordinary book on the subject of boy-girl relationships," he said. "This deals more with personal conduct on dates. It is intensely practical and is right where you live. It gives the Christian approach to the subject."

Danny looked about, allowing his gaze to rest first on one and then another.

"The first few pages deal with parent problems. But I suppose nobody here has ever had a problem with his parents."

A snicker rippled across the group.

A boy spoke up impetuously. "It probably tells us to mind our parents; that they know what they're talking about."

There was a short silence.

"I don't have the time to do it tonight, but I wish I could read you this chapter called 'Out of the Lab.' There's a lot of real meat in it for all of you. It takes examples from real life to show you what to look for in a guy or girl when you date and what pitfalls to avoid."

Danny flipped through a few more pages. "Now, here's a chapter that ought to interest a lot of you: 'Dating the Right Person.'"

Jim Morgan snorted. "The chapter I'm interested in is 'How Not to Date at All' or 'How to Keep the Girls Away.'"

Danny laughed with the others. "I seem to remember something about some beautiful lavender envelopes that came to you from Canada for a while after you got back this fall."

"Aw, can't a guy even write to a friend without having somebody go broadcasting it all over town? Besides, I can't write up there anymore."

"Why not?" Danny Orlis wanted to know. "Did somebody beat your time?"

"Naw, it was nothing like that. I lost the address."

It was almost a minute before the group quieted down so Danny could continue.

"You know, I'm afraid a lot of Christian kids don't realize just how important it is to date the right person. If you follow the advice given here, you can't go wrong."

"What does it say about dating a girl who isn't a Christian?" one boy asked.

"That's one subject it spends a great deal of time on. I'd suggest that you get a copy so you can find out."

Robin Evans spoke up. "Does–does it say anything about–about making out and things like that?"

Danny nodded. "In my estimation that is one of the most important chapters in the entire booklet. I'm not going to tell you what it says. I want you to read it. I'd like each of you to get a copy and study it thoroughly. Then, I'd like to have each one of you apply it in your lives. If you do, you'll solve some of the biggest problems you will ever face as a young person."

CHAPTER 7

JIM'S BURNOUT GAME

That night when the kids from Bible club finally went home, Danny Orlis turned to Kay. "How did that seem to go over? Do you think they were interested?"

"Oh, I think so. They were all real attentive, and as they went out, I heard several say they were going to buy the booklet."

Linda Penner shrugged her shoulders. "I know how to act on a date," she said. "I don't know why I'd have to buy their old book."

If Kay was shocked, she gave no sign. "I could tell you about a girl or two I used to go to school with, Linda. They thought they knew all about how to act on dates, too, and they weren't going to have anyone tell them anything. They ended up disgracing their families, hurting their parents terribly, and almost ruining their own lives."

The Penner girl's cheeks paled slightly. "What kind of a girl do you think I am?" she asked indignantly.

Danny spoke up. "That's really not the point, Linda. Every guy and girl should do some long, hard thinking on these things. If they would, a lot of them would spare themselves a good deal of heartache and grief."

Linda picked up the booklet thoughtfully, thumbed the pages, and laid it back on the end table.

* * *

The following afternoon Jim Morgan and Pat Dougal, the other student manager, were out on the football field waiting for the last practice session of the season to end. They were playing the final game the next night and the coaches were giving the squad a light workout in the brisk November air.

The youthful managers stomped up and down the sidelines, trying to keep warm. Finally Jim spied an old baseball that must have been lost on the field the summer before and picked it up. He looked at it for a moment and tossed it in the air.

Pat Dougal called for it. "Hey," he sang out. "Toss it here."

Jim threw it to him. Pat threw it back, a little harder.

"So that's what you want, is it?" Jim Morgan exclaimed. He drew back his arm and snapped the ball back to his friend.

It stung Pat's hand and he shook it to stop the tingling.

"If it's a game of burnout you want, you've come to the right guy," Pat announced.

"Burnout?" Jim echoed. "Without gloves? Are you out of your mind?"

Pat chuckled. "You're not chicken, are you?"

Each time they threw the ball they stepped back a pace or so until they were farther apart than the pitcher and catcher in a regular baseball game. Pat Dougal had a good strong arm and the ball whistled into Jim's reddened palms. He looked down at them gingerly and rubbed them on the sides of his pants. He drew back the ball and fired it in.

Pat gasped as he caught it. "Wow!" he cried, "you've really got an arm."

"What's the matter?" Jim called to him. "Have you had enough? Are you ready to admit that I burned you out?"

Pat shook his head doggedly. "Me, burned out? I'm just getting warmed up."

Jim Morgan had played quite a little baseball, but he had never tried to pitch. So he had never really tried to sizzle the ball in before. He drew back his arm, put his weight behind the throw, and rifled the ball to Pat. The student manager saw that it was blistering and let it go by.

Jim chortled gleefully. "I guess that does it, Pat. I'm the champ."

The other boy went to retrieve the ball. "A guy'd be crazy to try to catch a ball like that bare-handed. Who taught you to throw, anyway?"

"I know one thing," Jim laughed. "It wasn't you. I can burn you out any day in the week."

Neither boy realized they had an audience until the assistant coach called out. "Hey, Jim! Throw it here!"

The boy hesitated.

"Throw it to me."

Jim turned and fired the ball out to him in the center of the football field. Coach Hammond reached for it with his bare hands.

"Ouch!" he shouted involuntarily, dropping the ball. For a moment or two he rubbed his hands together. Then, quite deliberately, he picked up the baseball and came over to where Jim was standing.

"Here's your ball," he said quietly.

Jim's face flushed. "I–I found it here in the grass and we–we just got to playing catch with it," he managed.

The coach's expression did not change. "I want to see you in my office tomorrow morning at eight o'clock."

Jim Morgan felt the sweat come out on his forehead. "Yes, sir."

"I want you there at eight sharp. Do you understand?"

The boy nodded. "I–I'll be there."

"And don't be playing burnout without gloves. If you do, somebody's apt to get a broken finger."

When Coach Hammond was gone Pat Dougal

came over to where Jim Morgan was standing. His voice was thin and quavering, mirroring his concern. "I sure hope I didn't get you in a jam with Mr. Hammond," he said. "I'll go with you in the morning and tell him it was all my idea if you think it would do any good."

"Thanks," Jim Morgan said. "But there's no need for both of us getting into trouble. I'm already in trouble. I don't think it would do any good to get him mad at you, too."

"I know, but I don't like the idea of having you take the blame for something that's my fault, too."

There was a brief silence.

"He sure was mad at me, though. I thought for a couple of minutes that I was going to get clobbered."

Pat Dougal grinned. "If his hand stung like mine did, I don't think I'd blame him."

Jim wiped the sweat from his forehead. "Do you think he'll kick me off the team as student manager?"

"I sure don't think so. After all, you didn't ask him into the game. He saw us playing and told you to throw the ball to him."

Nevertheless Jim Morgan could think of little else that night. He had a history test to study for, but all he could think about was the look on Coach Hammond's face. And that certainly didn't make it any easier for him to study.

* * *

Tom Channing actually didn't have to go to the library to study that evening. But he heard Robin Evans say she was going to be there, so he dropped by just before closing time. She was sitting at one of the tables, books stacked around her.

"Hello," Tom said.

She put her finger to her lips in warning.

"Going home in a few minutes?" His voice lowered to a whisper.

She did not answer him.

"I'll wait outside for you, Robin."

At that moment the librarian came striding up to the end of the table and stared at him significantly.

"I–I was just going."

At nine o'clock Robin Evans came outside, her arms loaded with books. Tom was waiting for her on the sidewalk.

"I'm sorry for busting in like that and talking to you," he said. "I sure fouled things up for you. I hope old 'Eagle Eye' didn't give you a bad time when I was gone."

She smiled. "Oh, no," she said. "She just informed me that the library was a place to read and study, not to meet boyfriends and make dates."

"Did you tell her I was an uninvited guest?"

"To be honest with you, Tom, I didn't tell her anything. I just listened."

They both laughed.

"Would it be all right if I walked home with you?" he asked after a moment or two.

She paused uncertainly. "I don't think so, Tom." Her voice was kind but unmistakably firm.

His eyes widened.

"What's the matter? Am I poison or something?"

"It's not that," she answered. "In fact, I like being with you."

"Then what's wrong?" he demanded. "Why won't you go out with me?"

She turned to face him.

"I don't like having to tell you this, Tom," she said, "but you are entitled to an explanation. I do like being with you. I've had a lot of fun the times we've been together."

"Then why the sudden brush-off? It doesn't sound to me as though you've had so much fun. If you had, you wouldn't mind walking home with me."

"The trouble is that we have such different convictions about what should be done and shouldn't be done on a date that I don't feel it's best to go with you anymore."

Incredulously he stared at her. "Now wait a minute. You aren't trying to tell me that you won't go out with me because I tried to kiss you the other night, are you?"

"That's part of it."

His temper flared. "Where've you been all your life?" he asked irritably. "All the kids are doing it."

Her smile took some of the sting out of her words, but only added to her decisiveness.

"I only have to answer for myself, Tom. And I know that I can't do it and maintain my Christian testimony."

"What does it hurt to make out a little, as long as you don't go too far?" he demanded. "That's what I want to know."

"You were at Bible club the other night," she told him. "Have you read that booklet, *Dating Tips for Christian Teens,* that Danny was talking about?"

He shrugged indifferently. "Nope. I just figure that's some stuff a bunch of old fogies are trying to sell. They shouldn't tell us what we ought to do."

"I've got a copy of the booklet. My mother bought it for me. You read what it says and you'll find the answer to your question about what's wrong with a little making out."

His voice grew insistent. "You would go to church with me, wouldn't you, Robin?" he almost pleaded. "Or to the youth group banquet that is coming up in a couple of weeks? There wouldn't be anything wrong with that."

She shook her head.

"I'm sorry, Tom. Truly I am. But I think it's best if we just don't go together at all."

He shook his head incredulously.

"You don't really mean that, do you?"

"Yes, Tom, I do."

She looked at her watch. "It's getting late. I'm afraid I have to run now. Goodbye, Tom."

He looked after her as she turned the corner and disappeared from view. It was the first time he'd ever seen a girl like that who wouldn't go out with him just because he put his arm around her a couple of times and tried to kiss her. She was just odd.

Sorrowfully he turned and walked back home. It sure would be something to have a girl like Robin Evans, but there was no hope of that now. She would never go out with him again.

CHAPTER 8

CHANCE OF A LIFETIME

Thoughtfully Tom Channing retraced his steps back home. Robin Evans' quiet voice still echoed hauntingly in his ears. He knew that his cheeks were still flushed scarlet.

He was a Christian and could give as good a testimony as any of the kids his age at church. He didn't smoke or swear or do any of the things that their church frowned on, but that didn't seem to make a bit of difference to Robin Evans. She seemed to think he was as bad as Jack Ross or any of the other punks out at school. And all because of the way he acted on a date.

His lips tightened forcefully and, although he didn't notice, his pace quickened until he was striding purposefully through the chill November air.

That talk about getting upset because he tried to kiss her good night was just a line. She didn't want to go with him and used that as an excuse to make herself appear to be holy.

Either that or she was just weird and too old-fashioned. He could have told her something if he had wanted to hurt her. She wasn't so much fun on a date herself. In fact she was the biggest prude he'd ever had out.

He crossed the street and turned. As soon as word got around, she'd be finished as far as dating any of the guys out at school was concerned. Let her see how she'd like that. After she'd sat home for a couple of months, she'd begin to wish she had a chance to go out with him again and treat him a little nicer. She'd begin to change her tune.

At the intersection he paused to let a car go by in front of him. Jack Ross waved from the driver's seat at him.

Slowly Tom's thinking began to change. He was a Christian, all right. He had settled the matter years ago and had always felt that he was a little more dedicated than the average guy in his Sunday school class.

But had he honestly treated Robin as though he was letting Christ control his life? Would he want some guy to treat his sister the way he wanted to treat Robin? Would he want the girl he would marry someday to be treated that way by the other guys she had dated? The thought stabbed deep into his heart.

Without realizing quite what he was about, he turned and went over to Danny Orlis's home, where he knocked timidly.

Kay came to the door. "Why, hello, Tom," she said pleasantly. "Won't you come in?"

For a brief instant his face flushed, and he fought against a fierce desire to turn and flee.

"I wish I could," he managed, forcing out the words one by one. "But I don't have time for that tonight. I–I just came by to see if you had a copy of that little booklet Danny told us about at Bible club the other night."

"You mean *Dating Tips for Christian Teens?*" she asked.

He stepped just inside the door and closed it behind him. "I guess that's the name of it. The one Danny talked to us about at Bible club is the one I want to get hold of."

Kay turned away. "Just a minute, Tom. I think I can find it. I know we've got a copy of it around here somewhere."

Tom sat down uneasily on the edge of a chair.

"I was talking to Robin Evans this evening at the library," he said. "She told me she had just got her copy and had been reading it. From what she said it's pretty terrific."

Linda Penner, who had been in the other room studying, heard Tom's voice and came out where he was sitting. Her smile was coy and ingratiating.

"Hello, Tom," she trilled. "I didn't expect to see you here tonight."

"I didn't expect to be over here, either." He flushed self-consciously as Kay Orlis came back and handed him the booklet. "I was going by and decided to stop in and see if I could borrow the booklet Danny was telling us about at Bible club."

"I didn't think too much about it when Danny was talking," Linda Penner put in, "but when I got to reading it myself, I soon changed my mind. It has a lot of good advice in it for Christian young people."

Nodding, Tom shoved the booklet into his pocket and stood to leave.

"Thanks a lot, Kay. I'll bring it back in a couple of days."

"Oh, you won't have to do that, Tom. Keep it as long as you like. Danny was so impressed with it that he ordered several copies to have in case any of the kids came around and wanted to read it."

Although Tom Channing had only spoken to her briefly, and then in answer to a direct question, Linda followed him to the door. "Are you going to youth group banquet, Tom?"

He shrugged his shoulders indifferently. "I've thought about it some, but I don't know for sure. I don't go much for parties and banquets."

Linda Penner eyed him wistfully. "I would like to go," she murmured, hurt clouding her eyes. "But I don't know if I will get to go or not. There's no fun in going to a place like that alone and almost everyone who is planning to take a date has already got one."

"Maybe you could go with me," he said impulsively. He hadn't planned on asking her to go to the banquet.

After Robin indicated she wouldn't go out with him anymore he had decided he would either go alone or not go at all. But he hadn't reckoned on Linda. Now he had a date whether he wanted one or not.

Linda Penner's eyes sparkled her excitement. "Oh, Tom," she gasped. "That would be wonderful."

Slightly dazed by what had happened, Tom Channing said goodbye and left the house. The little booklet on dating weighed heavily in his hand.

* * *

The following morning Jim Morgan went to school half an hour early and stood in front of the coach's office a few minutes before eight. He paced back and forth uneasily and glanced at his watch every now and then. It seemed to take Mr. Hammond ages to get to his office, but actually he was only two or three minutes late.

"Hello, Jim," he said pleasantly. "I see you made it." He unlocked his office and stepped inside. Reluctantly Jim Morgan followed him.

Coach Hammond closed the door and walked around his desk to sit down.

"I called you in this morning, Jim, to see exactly what you can do with a baseball."

The boy's eyes widened.

"Tell me, have you ever done any pitching?"

"Me, pitch?" he echoed. "Are you kidding?"

"Not at all." He pursed his lips tightly. "You have

a good fastball, Jim. A very good fastball. I'd like to have you throw me a few so I can see whether that throw yesterday was an accident or not."

Jim's lower jaw sagged, but the words would not come out.

"Let's go down in the gym and see just what you can do."

The coach took a glove and catcher's mitt from the locker in one corner of his office and the two of them walked down the corridor to the gymnasium. The Morgan boy followed along behind numbly.

Once in the gymnasium, Coach Hammond tossed Jim the glove and ball.

"Go over there near the foul line," he said, "and throw to me. Put all the steam you've got on it."

The corners of the boy's mouth twitched.

"But, Coach, you–you got mad at me last night for throwing hard to you."

Coach Hammond laughed.

"I wasn't mad at you, Jim. I was just surprised, that's all. I didn't expect you to have such an arm on you."

He pulled on the catcher's mitt, bent his knees slightly, and called for the ball.

"Let's have it, Jim. And don't spare the horses."

Jim snapped the ball across the gym to Mr. Hammond. The coach scowled his displeasure.

"Come on. You can do better than that. I've got a five-year-old boy at home who can do a better job of throwing than that. Put some heat on it."

Jim Morgan gripped the ball tightly, drew back, and rifled it at the coach. It went wide but Mr. Hammond reached over and stabbed it with his mitt.

"That's a little better." He tossed the ball back to Jim. "Now let's try it again and give it everything you've got."

Jim came back on one foot, brought the ball forward with a powerful motion, and sent it sizzling in the direction of the coach. It was almost over Coach Hammond's head, but he caught it just the same. It thudded into his mitt resoundingly.

"Now, that's better," he said. "That's a lot more like what I thought we could expect from you."

Jim still had no idea what he was talking about.

"You've got the steam, Jim," Coach Hammond said. "You've got plenty of smoke on your fastball, only you don't seem to have much of an idea where it is going when you let loose of it."

Jim came over to him.

"I suppose that's right. I've never given much thought to where the ball was going when I threw."

Coach Hammond nodded.

"That's about the way I had it figured. If you pitch for us that way, you'll kill us with walks."

Jim gasped.

"Pitch? I don't know anything about pitching."

"You could learn," the coach said curtly. "You've got a lot of steam. If you could learn to control the ball, you'd be able to win a few games for us."

Jim Morgan was incredulous.

"Do–do you really mean it?"

"I certainly do," the coach replied. "All you've got right now is a lot of speed. And it's probably going to take a lot of work to teach you control and give you a good change of pace. But if you're willing to work at it – harder than you've ever worked at any sport before – I think we might have a chance of making a good pitcher of you."

Astonishment widened Jim's eyes. It still was almost impossible to believe.

"I'll work as hard as I can if I've got a chance of making the team."

"Now, wait a minute, Jim," Coach Hammond put in. "You might develop into a good pitcher and you might not. I've seen guys who could throw like you settle down and become good control pitchers. I've seen others who never did learn to find the plate. I can't make you any promises except that I'll do my best to teach you what I know if you'll do your best to put it into practice."

"That's a deal. If I've just got a chance, that's good enough for me." A wide grin broke across Jim's young face. "What do we do and when do we start?"

"If you don't have any eight o'clock classes, I think that will be as good a time for us to get together as any. We'll meet here in the gym and work out for forty-five minutes or so every morning at about eight o'clock."

"Sounds great!"

Jim Morgan was in a dream that morning when he left the gym. Imagine, he had a chance to pitch for Fairview High! Him! Jim Morgan! It wasn't real. It couldn't be.

Yet he knew full well that it was. Determination set his jaw. He didn't know whether he could master control well enough to make the grade, but if trying hard had anything to do with it, there wasn't any question. He'd make it, all right!

Jim Morgan and Coach Hammond began to work out together the following morning. They went down into the gym at eight o'clock and Jim threw as hard as he could, under Coach Hammond's direction, until it was time for them to quit and go to class. It was hard, grueling work, and Jim was so discouraged after the first session that he was almost ready to quit. He said nothing to the coach about it but talked with Danny that evening when he got home.

"I'm afraid it's a waste of the coach's time, Danny," he said, discouragement etched in his young face. "I don't think I'll ever be able to learn anything about pitching."

"That's no way to talk, Jim. Don't let it get you down."

"But you ought to see how wild I am. I don't think I'd ever be able to find the plate in a real game."

"Now wait a minute. You've got the natural ability to throw hard. That's something you could never hope to become a pitcher without. Control is often just a matter of mastering certain fundamentals.

And anyone can do that if they keep plugging away long enough and hard enough."

"I suppose you're right." He picked up his books and started for his room to study. Dejection was in his every movement. At the door he turned back. "Danny, I sure would appreciate it if you wouldn't say anything to anyone about what the coach and I are doing every morning. People will think that we're both crazy if they find out we're practicing baseball at this time of the year."

Danny Orlis laughed. "I won't say anything about it if you don't want me to," he agreed, "but I certainly don't think anyone will say you're crazy. If I were a coach, I'd be mighty glad I had a boy who wanted to play baseball badly enough to spend time every day all winter trying to learn to pitch."

There was a slight hesitation.

"But, Danny, do you think I've really got a chance of learning how to control the ball? Do you think I'll be good enough to get to pitch in some of the games?"

"All you can do is your best. If you put out everything you've got, you don't have anything to be ashamed of, Jim, regardless of what happens."

Jim started toward his room a second time, but once more he turned back. "You know, Danny," he said, "there's something else that's worrying me a little."

"Now, what's that?" Danny asked jokingly. "Don't tell me you've got girl problems."

"Oh, no, it's nothing like that."

He came back and sat down.

"Maybe this is silly," he began hesitantly. "But I keep thinking about Boyd Patterson."

Danny Orlis nodded. "What about Boyd?"

"He was the star pitcher for Fairview last year. He likes football and basketball all right, but the only sport he really is crazy about is baseball. He's always talking about how glad he'll be when we can start baseball practice."

"I know how he feels about the game," Danny answered. "But where's the problem?"

"He's my very best friend," Jim said, clenching his fists tightly. "What's he going to say when he finds out that I'm working as hard as I can to try and take his job away from him?"

Danny Orlis picked up a figurine on the end table and studied it thoughtfully.

"I can see that could develop into something of a problem with a guy who was apt to be a little jealous, Jim."

"I wouldn't even go out for baseball if I thought it would make him mad at me."

Danny was slow in answering him.

"I'm sure that's not the right answer either, Jim. You have the right to be on the team, too. And if you can pitch better than Boyd, then you ought to become the number one pitcher." He took a long breath and expelled the air slowly. "Of course, there's always room for more than one pitcher on a high school team, especially when one of them can hit as well as Boyd Patterson. It really depends on Boyd, Jim. If he's the kind of a guy who has to be the star – if he's got to have all the publicity and have people talking about what a great player he is – you might have some difficulty. If he's a regular guy who just wants to play ball and win games, everything will be all right."

Jim's frown deepened. Boyd didn't seem to be the kind of guy who would be jealous, but–

CHAPTER 9

"I HAVEN'T A THING TO WEAR!"

That evening Tom Channing went home and, after crawling into bed, lay there reading the little booklet he had gotten from Kay Orlis. The next few days he tried to get his mind off it, but he could not. At the oddest moments his thoughts would come back to it, and he found himself reading it again and again.

Somehow he had been able to force away most of the humiliation and hurt that came with Robin's frank refusal to go out with him, but it kept prying in at the corners of his heart. Belligerently he fought against it by arguing mentally with the authors on every page.

They were just old-fashioned, that was all. They tried to make so much out of just kissing a girl or putting your arm around her. The way they wrote they tried to make it sound as though it was some sort of a crime or something. They just didn't understand.

That was all. They didn't know what they were talking about. All the guys he knew did it. And so did most of the girls. Most of the ones he'd ever gone out with, that was, except Robin Evans. And she probably would have been all right if she hadn't gotten her hands on that book written by a bunch of crackpots. That was what did it.

Tom stopped thoughtfully, and for the space of a moment or two he could not get Robin out of his mind. He had to admit that he did respect and admire her. He had to admit that he longed to go out with her.

She wouldn't let him put his arm around her, but it was a cinch she didn't let anyone else get familiar, either. It would sure be something to have a girlfriend like that.

That evening, as soon as he had the opportunity, he got out the booklet and read it again. This time the belligerence in his attitude was gone.

He still wasn't too sure he agreed with everything in it. But a guy did have to give the authors credit. They wrote as though they knew what they were talking about. They knew how a guy thought and what the problems were. And what was more, they had answers to them.

Tom paused for a moment or two, staring across the room.

The booklet made sense. It made a lot of sense. If a guy and girl followed the advice given, a lot of them wouldn't get their lives in such messes, that was sure. And they'd probably be a lot happier, too.

He got to his feet and walked thoughtfully to the window. He knew now why he had found so much fault with the booklet the first time he had read it, why he had gotten so mad at the authors. It had been because he knew what they wrote was true. He hadn't liked it because he knew he would have to change his own ways if he let the booklet speak to his heart.

Tom paced back to the chair, picked up the little booklet, and held it.

He was a Christian, but he sure had a lot of cleaning up to do in his own life. He had sinned against the girls he had gone out with. He had sinned against God. Deliberately he sank to the floor and began to pray for forgiveness.

* * *

Over at the Orlis home, Linda Penner was in her own room too, sitting before the mirror on the dresser, excitement bright in her eyes. She was going to the youth group banquet with Tom Channing. He had actually asked her instead of Robin. She was the one he wanted to go with. Just let Jim Morgan try to tease her again!

Linda's smile was pensive and thoughtful. Jim acted as though he didn't like to be around her, but she had a feeling that he was more than a little jealous. That was the reason he acted the way he did.

She picked up a brush and ran it through her soft black hair. She could just hear the kids at school when she and Tom Channing came to the banquet. Everybody would be watching them, and the girls would just die of envy. They'd positively *die!*

Her smile faded.

She hadn't even thought of it before, but she would have to have a new dress for the banquet. That was all there was to it. She didn't have a thing to wear for going out on a date with a guy like Tom.

She went to her closet and opened it. It was filled with dresses, but she wrinkled her nose at them. They were just Sunday dresses and school dresses. She didn't have anything that was really nice. Nothing special that she had never worn before.

Linda went back to the dresser and sat down before the mirror. Already she had decided she had to have a new dress. Just how to get it was something of a problem. It was going to take some doing, that was sure.

For several minutes she sat there, thinking hard. She'd have to talk to Kay when Danny wasn't at home. It wouldn't do any good to bring up anything like getting a new party dress when he was there. Getting it would take a little doing.

And she wouldn't dare to say anything in front of Jim Morgan. He'd chime in with some stupid wisecrack that would ruin everything. Thoughtfully she began to brush her hair again.

She would have to talk to Kay about it, but she wasn't even sure that she would go along with it. She was *so* old-fashioned about anything like that. But there were times when she was a little understanding. She'd just have to take a chance and hope she was catching Kay in the right mood.

When Linda Penner got home the following evening, Kay Orlis was sitting alone in the living room. Becky was visiting a little neighbor girl, and neither Danny nor Jim had gotten home yet. She went over to Kay's chair and sat down on the arm.

"Did you know that there's going to be a youth group banquet at church next week?" she asked carefully.

Kay nodded. "I saw the announcement in the bulletin Sunday."

Linda smiled her winsomest. "Tom Channing has asked me to go with him."

Kay smiled her approval. "How nice."

Linda's smile faded slowly. "Only I'm not at all sure whether I can go or not," she said, sorrow edging her voice.

"It's certainly all right if you go with Tom Channing," Kay told her. "If that is what you're wondering about."

Linda allowed her frown to deepen, and her lower lip began to quiver slightly.

"That isn't the big problem, Kay," she managed. "I know you would approve of such a fine Christian boy as Tom. But the trouble is that I'm afraid I can't go because I don't have anything to wear."

Kay put aside the paper she had been reading. "I know just how you feel," she said. "I used to feel the same way when I was in high school and had a chance to go to something special."

Linda Penner brightened.

"Then I can get a new dress?" she asked.

"What about the lovely new dress your dad got you a couple of weeks ago?"

The high schooler shrugged her shoulders indifferently.

"Oh, that. I've already worn it to church dozens of times. It isn't new anymore. It's old and I'm not going to wear it."

Kay's voice was even and understanding.

"I think you're exaggerating the situation, Linda," she said. "I helped serve the banquet a year ago. As I recall it isn't particularly fancy – at least as far as the clothes the girls wear are concerned. They just wore their regular Sunday dresses."

Hurt flickered in Linda's dark eyes and just the right amount of disappointment tinged her voice.

"Maybe it was that way a year ago," she countered, "but it's not going to be that way this year. The girls I've talked with are all getting new dresses. None of them will be wearing clothes they've worn to Sunday school and church before. I–I'll be the only one in an old rag."

Kay did not reply.

"This is one of the biggest affairs of the whole year, Kay," Linda continued. "The kids all say that it–it's almost as important as the prom."

Kay Orlis reached up and took her hand gently. "I know exactly how you feel," she said understandingly. "I've felt the same way when something special is going on and I want to look my very best."

"Then I can get the dress?" Linda broke in quickly.

"I didn't say that. The money your dad left with us for clothes is about gone and Becky has to have a new pair of shoes this week."

She paused momentarily.

"I'll tell you what I'll do, Linda. I have some lovely material that would make a darling dress for you. Why don't we go down tomorrow afternoon and get a nice pattern? I'll help you make a new dress."

Linda Penner's countenance fell. "Make a dress?" she echoed. "Make a dress for a banquet? I've never heard of such a thing."

"I used to live on the mission field in Mexico, my dear," Kay went on. "Mom and I had to do all of our own sewing if we wanted any new clothes. You know I make most of my clothes now. And you sew very nicely yourself. Together we could make you a beautiful new dress."

Linda's eyes softened slightly, but disapproval was still etched on her attractive young face.

"Perhaps it would be all right for us to make a school dress," she said, "or even something to wear to church." She wrinkled her nose disdainfully. "But for a banquet dress? No, thank you. I'd rather not have a new dress at all than one that was homemade."

Kay Orlis picked up her paper once more. "Well, you can suit yourself, Linda. If you'd like to make a dress and want me to help you, I'll be glad to. If you don't want a handmade dress, that's all right, too."

Linda's lips curled into a pout and began to quiver. "I should have known you wouldn't understand," she complained bitterly. "Nobody around here understands. Nobody cares whether I have a good time at the banquet or not." Her voice caught and she swallowed hard. "Nobody even cares if I go."

Tearfully she forced out the words. "I'll show you whether I get a new dress or not, Kay Orlis. If you won't help me, I'll go to Daddy and talk with him. He'll get me a dress. He always gets me anything I want."

* * *

That same afternoon Tom Channing was waiting on the front steps at school for Robin Evans. When she finally came out, he went over to her.

"Hello, Tom." She was as friendly and as gracious as she had ever been to him.

"Hello, Robin." He fumbled uncertainly for words. "I wonder if I–I could talk with you for a couple of minutes."

"Certainly."

She took two or three steps to one side so the other kids couldn't hear what was being said.

"Robin," he began, "I know you told me that you don't want to go out with me, and I sure don't blame you for that, but I–" He glanced at the kids who were going by. "I've got to talk to you, but I can't do it here. Could I–I w-w-walk home with you just this once?"

Refusal stood on her tongue, but something about the earnest look in his eyes stopped her.

"Why, of course, Tom."

He smiled at her halfheartedly.

"Here, let me carry your books."

They had walked a block and a half or two blocks before he could bring himself to speak.

"I've been reading that little booklet, *Dating Tips for Christian Teens,*" he said. "I borrowed a copy of it from Danny and Kay."

"Isn't it good?"

"I didn't like it at first," he replied frankly. "To tell you the truth, the first time I read it through it made me good and mad."

She eyed him quizzically. "That seems strange to me. There isn't anything in it to make anyone mad. It's written to help us."

"I know that – now. The Lord really dealt with me through that little booklet. He made me see how wrong I've been."

There was a short silence.

"He made me see that there is a whole area of my life that I have to clean up," he continued miserably.

He stopped and turned to face her.

"I straightened it out with the Lord last night before I went to bed, Robin. That's why I had to see you today."

The lines about her eyes deepened.

"I don't believe I understand."

He swallowed hard. "I not only sinned against God; I sinned against you and the other girls I dated by not treating you as a Christian should treat his date." His gaze met hers – seriously. "I'm terribly sorry, Robin. Will you forgive me?"

"Of course I will." Her face softened measurably.

"I–I don't suppose it would do me any good to ask you this, Robin, but I–I'd sure like to go out with you again, if you would trust me."

Her smile was warm and reassuring. "I'd like to go out with you again, Tom," she said with disarming frankness. "The only reason I didn't want to go out with you in the first place was because of–of what you wanted to do when we were alone together. Now that God has taken care of that in your life I'd like to go with you once in a while."

A smile broke across his young face. "That's great. That's wonderful. I sure didn't think anything like this would ever happen. I–I–"

Jim Morgan, who was riding by on his bike just then, slowed and swerved close to them. "Don't get so upset, old man. You sound as though you're about to blow a gasket."

CHAPTER 10

LINDA'S STRATEGY

Linda Penner waited until the following week to go to her dad about getting her a new dress. Everything had to be just right. She kept waiting for a good opportunity, but for some reason it didn't come. Finally, time ran out until she could wait no longer. She had to go and talk to him whether the time was right or not.

When she came up to the back porch that evening Mr. Penner was sitting at the kitchen table. By the dim light she could see that he was going over his checking account, his sallow face lined and haggard. Suddenly Linda realized how very tired he looked and how much older. A dagger stabbed into her heart.

Nevertheless he smiled indulgently when she opened the door and came in.

"Hi, Daddy," she exclaimed brightly.

"Hello, Linda." He put his arm around her and kissed her tenderly.

"I've been so lonesome for you I just had to come over and see you."

She pulled up a chair and sat down.

"I only wish I was staying over here taking care of you the way I used to," she continued. "That is the thing that would make me happiest of all."

The frown lines in his forehead grew deeper. "We've been all over that, my dear. You know why we can't take you and Becky from Danny and Kay Orlis – at least right now."

Smiling, she nodded.

"I know that, Daddy, and I didn't come over here to argue with you about it. I know you're doing what you think is best for us, and we're both willing to stay over there as long as you want us to."

He relaxed a little. "I'm glad you understand that, Linda. It makes everything a great deal easier."

She pulled the chair closer to her father.

He eyed her knowingly. "Well," he said, "what is it this time?"

Disappointment pulled at the corners of her mouth. "What do you mean?"

He laughed gently. "What is it you want this time?"

"Daddy, don't talk that way," she scolded. "You make it sound as though I only come to see you when I want something from you."

He patted her on the shoulder. "That's all right, my dear. I'm used to it now."

It was a moment or two before she spoke. "After

having you talk that way to me," she said, "I hate to say anything to you about it, but there is something that I need awfully bad."

Her eyes met his and held them pleadingly.

"They're having a youth banquet at church this week, and–and all the other girls will have new dresses to wear and–" Her voice trailed away.

Henry Penner picked up a pencil and examined it momentarily before he replied. "I wish I could get you a new dress, Linda. I guess I wish I could buy you everything you would like to have, or even think you'd like. But to tell you the truth, I'm in a terrific financial bind right now. I was just going over my bank account to see if I'd have money enough to pay off my obligations the first of the month. I just don't have the money to buy a dress or anything else right now."

Her eyes clouded. "But Daddy!"

"I'm sorry, Linda, honey. Honestly, I am. And I wish there was something I could do about it. But there isn't. I can't help at all."

There was a short hesitation and her lower lip curled.

"I just won't go to the banquet then," she retorted petulantly. "I'll call them and tell them I have to stay home."

"But that's not true, Linda," he protested. "You don't have to stay home. You can go if you wish."

"I can't go without a new dress," she said, "so I'm not going. If you don't care whether I have any fun, it's all right with me. I'd think you would want me to go to the youth group banquet. I'd think you would be glad I'm taking an interest in things like that."

Henry Penner sighed deeply. "I am glad you are interested in going to some of the activities of the church, and I wish I could get you a new dress, Linda. But right now that's out of the question. I'm sorry."

By the tone of his voice she knew there was no use in arguing with him further.

That night Linda Penner determined to see Tom Channing and tell him she couldn't go to the banquet with him. But that was something she could not do. If she did, he'd only get a date with another girl and she would never have another chance to go out with him again.

She got out all of her old dresses and examined them critically, one by one. There just wasn't a thing in her closet that was fit to wear any place, let alone to a banquet. All she had was rags. Rags!

* * *

Linda hadn't planned to go into Maybelle's Dress Shop. In fact, she hadn't even wanted to go by it. But she did and, before she realized exactly what she was doing, she had gone inside.

That was a foolish thing to do, she told herself.

She didn't have any money to buy a dress. There was no use in even looking – especially in an expensive place like Maybelle's. She was just about to leave when she spied a darling dress on the rack just inside the door. She held it up to herself. It would fit perfectly. She just knew it would.

The clerk came over and insisted that she try it on.

"It does look beautiful on you."

Linda Penner's eyes sparkled. "Do you really think so?"

"It's positively darling. And the color is just right for you. It does something to your hair."

Linda's eyes widened and she turned reluctantly from the mirror. "I–I suppose I'll have to take it off now."

"Would you like to have me wrap it for you?" the clerk asked.

Linda shook her head. "I'd love to have it, but I–I'd have to have Dad come in and see it first."

The clerk read the disappointment in her eyes. "If you'd like, you can take it home on approval and see how he likes it tonight."

Linda's eyes widened. "Could I?"

"We would have to have it back tomorrow if you decide not to keep it. But you could do that, couldn't you?"

"Oh, yes. I'd bring it back tomorrow afternoon right after school–if–if I couldn't keep it."

The clerk wrapped it for her.

Triumphantly Linda Penner took the dress home and tried it on. She modeled it before the mirror. It was absolutely beautiful. It would be the most beautiful dress at the banquet. There was no doubt about that.

She raised a hand to pat her hair into place.

The clerk was right. The dress did something for her. She was still standing before the mirror when Kay Orlis came to the bedroom door and called to her.

"Linda," she said, "may I come in?"

For an instant panic seized the girl. Then she threw back her shoulders defiantly. "I was just coming out. I've got something to show you."

"I thought I'd see if I could–" Kay stopped suddenly. "Linda! Where did you get that dress?"

With tantalizing slowness Linda allowed a thin smile to play on her lips. "I told you that Daddy would get me a new dress when he found out what I had to wear to the banquet tonight."

Kay looked at it appraisingly.

"Do you like it?"

"It's lovely, and you make it even lovelier."

The dark-haired girl dimpled. "Thank you."

Linda Penner finished dressing excitedly and at 6:30 she went to the banquet with Tom Channing.

Linda Penner had thought she would have a wonderful time that evening, especially when the other girls started coming up to her and talking to her about the beautiful dress she was wearing. She tried to act as though it meant little to her, even when one of the girls positively raved about it.

"I wanted this dress worse than anything, Linda," she said. "I went into Maybelle's every afternoon for a couple of weeks. I even tried it on two or three times, but it was so expensive my parents wouldn't let me get it."

Linda tossed her shoulders indifferently. "I told Daddy that I didn't want him to get me such an expensive dress; but when he saw it on me, he just wouldn't let me try on anything else. He said I had to have it – that it was made just for me."

The other girl eyed her enviously. "I wish my parents were like that."

The color surged up into Linda's cheeks. For some reason the rest of the banquet didn't seem to be nearly so much fun after that. And when it was over, she was glad to start back home.

Tom Channing got her coat. "The banquet was great, wasn't it?" he asked.

She smiled up at him. "I thought it was wonderful."

They started for the car.

"You know," Tom went on, "that message really got hold of me. A guy has to face up to the claims of Christ on his life. There's no getting around it."

Linda nodded. "I thought the music was beautiful. I could sit and listen to Mr. Merrick sing all evening."

It was almost as though Tom had not even heard what she said.

"I'd never really considered the fact that Christ has a claim on the life of each of us," he went on. "He bought us and paid for us with His blood. We're going to have to answer to Him."

She nodded, annoyed by the darts that burrowed into her heart.

"And what is a guy who hasn't accepted Christ

going to say when he dies and stands before God?" Tom asked. "You know, he isn't going to be able to say a word. He'll stand condemned."

The words drove into Linda's heart. What she had done – as far as sinning was concerned – didn't amount to so much. You could practically say that she had never sinned at all. Or at least that was what Linda Penner tried to tell herself as they rode home. Still, the dull, nagging ache continued to grow in her heart.

"I don't think I've ever had a message get hold of me the way that one did. It made me want to grab every guy I meet and talk to him about the Lord."

The way Tom kept talking about the speaker and what he had said, Linda was almost glad when he took her home. At least she wouldn't have to listen to him preach at her anymore.

When she got home, she took off the dress, folded it carefully, and put it back in the box. The following morning she sneaked it out of the house, and on the way home from school stopped in at Maybelle's with it. The clerk who had waited on her came up to the counter.

"Didn't your dad like the dress, Linda?" she asked.

"He liked it all right," she replied, "but he thought it was a little too expensive." The lie caught in her throat. "He told me I'd better bring it back. I–I feel so sick about it that I could cry."

The clerk was very understanding. "That's quite all right," she said. "This sort of thing happens quite often. As long as the dress hasn't been worn, Maybelle won't object at all."

Linda Penner's cheeks flushed with guilt. "I–I put it on to show Daddy how it looked on me."

"We would expect that. I was talking about something entirely different – like wearing it to a party or for an entire evening." She turned back to the rack. "Is there something else we can show you? We have a large selection of dresses that are less expensive than this one."

Linda pretended to consider it for a moment or two. "I don't believe I'd better right now. I think I'll wait a little while and see if I can talk Dad into coming down here with me. If I can get him into the store, he'll see how much prettier this dress is than all the others. Perhaps I can still get him to buy it for me."

In a few minutes Linda was out of the store and on her way home. For a moment or two panic had shaken her, but things had worked out all right. She sighed her relief. That hadn't been so bad. It hadn't really been bad at all. She wore the dress, took it back, and nobody was hurt.

That was a good trick to remember. She might want to try it again sometime if she got into another spot like that.

It was almost 5:30 when Linda finally went into the Orlis home. Kay was sitting in the living room in a good dress, her coat over a chair.

Linda Penner looked at her curiously. "Why, hello,

Kay," she said brightly. "Did you just get home, or are you about to go out somewhere?"

Kay's lips were drawn tight, and her face was ashen. "You and I are going somewhere, Linda. Maybelle's Dress Shop called a few minutes ago."

Linda Penner's throat tightened, and fear leaped to her eyes.

CHAPTER 11

PAYDAY

For the space of a minute or two, stark terror reflected in Linda Penner's face.

"Wh-what did Maybelle want?" she asked hesitantly.

Kay's gaze met hers without wavering. "They want to talk to you, Linda."

Linda moistened her lips. "What do they want to talk to me about?"

There was a brief silence.

Like an icy shadow, fear swept through Linda Penner. "I–I–"

Kay's voice was flat and expressionless. "There's no need for you to say any more, Linda. They *know* you wore that dress last night."

Terror continued to gleam in Linda's eyes as she stared at Kay Orlis and her breath tore from her lungs in long, agonizing sobs.

"I–I didn't know I wasn't supposed to wear the

dress," she said lamely. "I thought it would be all right if I was really careful and didn't get the dress dirty or anything."

Kay's lips were set in a grim line and her voice was hard and brittle. "Now, Linda, don't make things any worse than they are already by lying. You told me that your dad had bought the dress for you. If you hadn't known it was wrong, you would have told me the truth."

The girl's mouth puckered. "That was because I–I thought you would scream at me," she alibied. "I didn't think the store would say anything. You have to believe me!" She was near tears.

"We don't have time to talk now, Linda. Maybelle is waiting for us." Her voice was soft and well-controlled, but there was a sternness in it that Linda had never heard before. "Come."

Kay Orlis slipped into her coat and ushered Linda out to the car.

Maybelle Kramer must have been watching for Kay Orlis and Linda Penner, for she met them at the door.

"You–you wanted to–to talk to me?" Linda gasped.

"I think we had better go back to my office."

Miss Kramer closed the door behind them and turned to face Linda Penner sternly. For the space of a full minute no one spoke.

"I–I didn't know I wasn't supposed to wear that dress to the banquet last night," Linda blurted desperately. "I didn't plan on wearing it. I just tried it on to see if it fit and it looked so nice on me that I–I felt I had to–to wear it. I'm terribly sorry. I wouldn't have done it if I'd known you cared. I–I'll never do it again."

Disbelief stood full in the store manager's eyes. Her expression did not change. "Now, Linda," she began, "don't ask me to believe that. I know better. This sort of thing is done all too often by too many women and girls. They do it for the same reason you did. They want a new dress for a special occasion, but they either don't want to spend the money for it or don't have the money. In either case, they are stealing from the store owner."

"But I–" Linda protested.

"I know very well what you intended to do, Linda," Maybelle continued. "You thought you could return the dress and we would never find out that it had been worn."

Linda Penner moistened her lips uncertainly, but she did not speak.

"What do you intend to do about it?"

"I–I–"

Kay broke in quietly. "What do you think should be done, Maybelle?"

There was a brief silence.

"I haven't talked this over with you, Mrs. Orlis, but frankly, I feel that since Linda wore the dress, she ought to buy it."

The girl's eyes widened, and a gasp escaped her lips. "Buy it?" she echoed. "I–I would never be able to get enough money to pay for a dress like that. It's so terribly expensive that–that–"

"It is an expensive dress," the store owner admitted. "It is very expensive. You should have thought of that before you took it out on approval and wore it."

"But you got the dress back. I didn't hurt it."

Maybelle nodded. "You are quite right. The dress hasn't been hurt. In fact, after it is cleaned it will be as good as new. However, you wore the dress where it was seen by a large number of people. That makes it almost impossible for us to sell it to anyone who lives in Fairview."

"I–I see," Linda answered numbly.

"As far as your having the money to pay for it is concerned, that won't make any difference one way or another. I won't accept money for it."

Linda Penner straightened suddenly. "What do you mean?"

"I am going to insist that you work it out. This is our busiest season of the year. I am going to expect you to work for me every Saturday afternoon and any other time I call on you until the dress is completely paid for."

The hurt in the girl's young face deepened.

"What do–do you expect me to do?"

"I need a girl for our stockroom," Maybelle said. "Someone to unpack dresses, help with the gift wrapping, and so on. According to our regular wage scale, you should have the dress paid for in about a month." The store owner turned to Kay. "Does that sound fair to you, Mrs. Orlis?"

"I think you're being very generous," Kay told her.

Linda Penner swallowed hard. "I–I don't mind

working for the dress, but do I have to work in the stockroom?" she pleaded. "Couldn't I work out front?"

The store manager shook her head. "We will be hiring a girl to help wait on customers, but we couldn't use you for that, Linda. Our clerks must be honest."

The Penner girl's lips trembled.

As she and Kay left the store her eyes brimmed with tears. "I–I don't think I'll be able to go back to school again, Kay," she said brokenly. "Everyone will find out what I did. The story will spread all over town and the kids will all be laughing at me."

"That's the way it is with sin," Kay reminded her. "Sooner or later it's always found out."

"But you don't know what it's like to have everyone talking about you."

They got into the car and Kay Orlis started the engine.

"There is one thing about what has happened that bothers me a great deal, Linda," she said slowly. "Listening to you I get the distinct impression that your chief concern isn't with what you've done. I think you are ashamed because you got caught and everyone will know about it. That isn't real repentance at all."

Linda Penner wiped her eyes defiantly "You talk to me as though I just robbed a bank or something. All I did was use the dress for one evening. I took it back to the store and now I'm going to have to work for ages and ages just to pay for it. I don't think I've done anything so terrible."

"As far as last night is concerned," Kay reminded her, "you stole that dress."

"Well, you don't need to talk as though I'm a criminal or something. I'm sorry for what I did, and I'm going to pay for it."

They reached the house, but it was several minutes before they went inside.

"Linda, I don't want to preach to you all the time, but you have been going your own way ever since you came to live with us, and it has caused you nothing but trouble. Won't you try the Lord's way?"

Linda Penner did not reply.

* * *

Linda worked the first Saturday afternoon and hated every minute of it. Maybelle had just received a huge shipment of dresses. Linda had to unpack them all, put them on hangers, and hang them up according to lot numbers. While she worked, she could hear the other girls talking pleasantly with their customers.

That was the way it always went, she reasoned. No matter what happened she got the worst end of everything. Like right now. She was slaving away in the back room while everyone else was having fun up front. It wasn't fair at all.

When she finished working, Maybelle came out to the back room.

"You've done a nice job today, Linda," she said. "I'm pleased with your work."

The girl's lips curled. "I'd like it a lot better if I could be up front waiting on customers."

"Perhaps you would." Maybelle's voice tightened. "I just thought I'd tell you that we will be unpacking more spring dresses and marking them next Friday night. I'd like to have you come down then."

"But that's–" she started to protest.

"We will be starting at six-thirty. I'll expect you here then."

Friday night was the night of the winter athletic banquet. Tom Channing hadn't asked her to go with him yet, but she knew that he was going to. She just knew it! And she wouldn't be able to go. A tear trembled on her eyelashes.

Now Tom would find out about the dress, and she'd never be able to face him again.

* * *

Sure enough, Sunday after church Tom came over to where Linda was standing. "Oh, there you are. I've been looking all over for you."

Linda forced a thin smile. "I had to go downstairs and get my coat."

"I wanted to talk to you about the athletic banquet. Will you go with me?"

The hurt stood in her eyes. "I'm sorry, Tom. I'd really like to go with you, but I–I can't."

The smile left his face. "I wish you could go with

me. They're going to give me some kind of an award for football."

"You don't know how bad it makes me feel, Tom," she said, tears trembling in her voice.

"Why can't you go with me?"

Her cheeks flushed and her gaze lowered slowly.

"Have you got another date?" he persisted.

"It isn't anything like that," Linda said. "It–it–well, it's Kay Orlis. She'll never let me do anything I want to do! Sometimes I think she hates me!"

Tom's face darkened. "If that's all the trouble, I don't think you've got a thing to worry about."

"Wh-what do you mean?"

"You'll find out soon enough."

Before she could protest further, he whirled on his heel and stormed away.

That evening after church, Danny Orlis was sitting in the living room when Tom Channing came over to the house.

"Hello, Tom," he said pleasantly. "How are you?"

The boy came into the house and stood uneasily just inside the door.

"Won't you sit down?"

"If it's all the same to you," Tom Channing retorted, "I'd just as soon stand."

He drew himself up to his full height and looked straight at Danny Orlis. "This is none of my business, I know, but I–I don't think you're being fair with Linda."

The young missionary's expression did not change.

"I know you're trying to take care of her the way her dad would, but the athletic banquet is one of the biggest affairs of the year," Tom continued. "I don't think it's right to punish Linda by making her stay home."

Danny Orlis stared at him blankly.

CHAPTER 12

TOM'S DISCOVERY

There was a brief, tense silence.

Danny stared at Tom Channing. "I think you must have been badly misinformed, Tom. We haven't told Linda she couldn't go to the football banquet with you. In fact, this is the first I've even heard about it."

Disbelief mingled with indignation in Tom Channing's eyes. "That's not the way I got it from Linda," he said firmly.

Danny's frown deepened. "I can't imagine why Linda would tell you anything like that, Tom. We don't object to your dating her. If she wants to go to the banquet with you, it's all right with us. We have no objections."

The boy stood his ground. "I don't get it, Danny. I don't get it at all. I talk to Linda, and she tells me that you and Kay won't let her go anywhere that night, even though you know it is the night of the athletic banquet. Now I talk to you, and you say that as far as you're concerned, she can go. Just what gives?"

Tom took a deep breath and expelled the air with a rush.

"I was going over to talk to her dad about it," he said before Danny had an opportunity to speak, "but I don't know him very well, so I decided to come over and see you about it first. You're not her father, Danny. I don't think it's fair for you to punish Linda by not letting her go to the banquet with me."

Danny Orlis turned. "I think you and I had better get to the bottom of this, Tom," he said. "There are some things I don't understand, either."

He moved toward the kitchen. "Kay," he called, "would you and Linda please come in here for a minute?"

They came into the living room and spoke to Tom.

Danny was stern and unsmiling. "Kay, Tom has a question he would like to ask you."

Desperation gleamed in Linda's eyes and her lips parted.

"I came over here to–" he began lamely.

Quickly the dark-haired girl broke in. "Don't say anything more, Tom. Let's just skip it. I don't want to make a scene or have any more trouble. It's all over and done with."

"But I–" he protested.

"It's all right. Let's just forget it." She went over to him, trying to smile reassuringly through her fears. "I looked for you after school tonight to tell you something, but I–I couldn't find you."

He shook away her feeble attempt to change the subject. "You can pass over it if you want to, but I'm not going to," he said hotly. Anger flecked his eyes. "You're getting a raw deal over here, and I'm not going to stand for it. If your dad won't step in and get things straightened out, it's time that somebody else does. I've never heard of anything as unfair as keeping you away from the football banquet just because you did something that Kay Orlis didn't happen to like."

Kay looked from Tom to Linda, whose cheeks were a deep scarlet. "I'm completely at a loss to know what you're talking about, Tom. It sounds to me as though someone has told you that we've forbidden Linda to go to the athletic banquet with you, but that's not true. We didn't even know there was going to be an athletic banquet, let alone forbid Linda to go to it."

Tom Channing's mouth sagged open slightly and his hands relaxed and clenched in rhythm. Slowly he turned and directed his attention to Linda.

"Somebody gave me that information," he said, "and I'm not standing very far away from her."

Linda's mouth worked nervously. "I–I didn't m-m-mean it quite the-the-the-way it–" Her voice trailed off into nothingness.

With that Danny Orlis took over. "Linda," he said sternly, "it's quite apparent that you have told Tom something about Kay and me. I think you owe him and us an explanation. Just what is this all about? Why did you tell him that we wouldn't let you go to the athletic banquet with him when it wasn't true?"

"I–I–" Tears trickled down her cheeks and she jumped to her feet and started for her bedroom.

"Linda!" Danny called out firmly. "Come back here and sit down."

She stopped at the bedroom door but did not turn back immediately.

"Come in here, Linda," Danny repeated, his voice rising. "We want to talk to you."

Slowly she turned and began to move mechanically toward them. Danny did not speak again, but his eyes forced her to do as he ordered. Meekly she came back to her chair and sat down. Sobs still shook her frail young shoulders spasmodically.

"And while you're at it," he said coldly, "stop that bawling. We want to talk to you."

She sniffled momentarily and wiped her eyes.

"Now," Danny began, "suppose you start from the beginning and tell us everything. Just what is this all about?"

Linda started to cry once more, but a stern glance in her direction from Danny Orlis stopped her.

"Well, it's this way," she said. "I–I've been working in the stock room at Maybelle's, and she said that I–I had to w-w-work Friday night." Her gaze met Tom's miserably.

Disgust clouded the boy's eyes. "Well, if that was

the reason," he exclaimed, "why didn't you tell me that in the first place? Why did you lie to me so I'd come over and–and make a big fool of myself to Danny?"

She struggled to find words. "I–I was afraid that you–you wouldn't understand."

"There's one thing I can't understand," he retorted hotly. "That's your reason for lying to me. All you'd have had to do would have been to tell me you had to work. That sort of thing happens all the time."

He pulled on his coat and stood self-consciously before Danny and Kay.

"I–I'm terribly sorry I came over here and mouthed off to you the way I did, Danny. I–I sure didn't act the way a Christian ought to act." He was biting his lower lip. "Will–will you forgive me?"

A big smile lit Danny's face as he thrust out his hand. "Sure thing, Tom."

When Tom Channing was gone, Linda Penner stared after him numbly. It was several minutes before she could speak.

"He–he'll never go out with me again," she murmured miserably. "He'll never go out with me again."

Danny turned to her, disgust flaming in his eyes. "Why should he go out with you, Linda?"

Her gaze met his. "I suppose you think I'm the worst person on earth right now, just because I told a little white lie."

"You still didn't tell him the truth, Linda. You only told him part of it."

Horror gleamed in her eyes. "But I couldn't tell him everything that happened," she protested. "I just couldn't!"

Still trembling uncertainly, she got to her feet.

"You know, Linda, I'm sure you would feel much better if you had told Tom the truth right from the start. It's always best to tell the truth – even though it sometimes hurts terribly to do so."

She tried to answer him, but she could not. It was a full minute before she spoke again.

"Is–is it all right if I–I go to my room now?" she asked quietly.

He nodded. "I am sorry things worked out for you the way they did. If you had told Tom the whole story, I'm sure you would have found that he was on your side."

She burst into tears and fled to the safety of her bedroom. The door slammed behind her, and she threw herself on the bed, crying uncontrollably.

Kay Orlis turned to Danny. "Do you think I ought to go in and talk to her?"

"It might be all right," he said. "She's terribly upset."

Kay entered Linda Penner's bedroom and closed the door quietly behind her.

"Linda," she said softly.

There was no answer.

"Linda."

"Go way and leave me alone."

Instead of leaving the room, Kay Orlis sat down on the side of the bed and put her arm about the distraught girl. Linda buried her head in Kay's lap, her young shoulders shaking convulsively. Kay made no attempt to speak or even to stop her crying. However, in a short while Linda began to get control of herself. She stopped her sobbing and looked up, wiping at her eyes.

"Oh, Kay, I–I don't know what's the matter with me," she blurted. "I don't want to tell things th-that aren't true and cause everyone all sorts of trouble all the time. I don't want to do any of the things I do, but I–I just can't help it."

Kay nodded understandingly. "That's exactly right, Linda. You can't help sinning. Neither can I or anyone else. We need God's help in order to live the way we should."

The girl started to sniffle again.

"God wouldn't want me," she sobbed. "I'm no good. I could never amount to anything for Him."

Kay's voice was kind and gentle.

"Do you know what the Bible has to say about that?" she asked. *"For I will be merciful to their unrighteousness, and their sins and iniquities will I remember no more.* All you have to do, Linda, is to recognize that you are a sinner and put your trust in the Lord Jesus Christ to save you, and He will. It doesn't make any difference who you are or what you've done or haven't done."

Linda Penner started to cry again. "I'm not going back to school anymore, Kay." Her voice broke plaintively. "Tom Channing won't go out with me anymore now that he knows I–I lied to him. He–he'll tell the other kids and I–I'll be the laughingstock of the whole school."

Kay selected her words with care. "I don't think Tom is the kind to tell anyone anything about you, Linda. But that isn't really important."

"It is to me."

"The important thing is for you to get your whole life straightened out, my dear. Sin is your big problem. Sin has got a stranglehold on you, just as it has on all of us before we trust Christ as our Savior. And what is worse, its grip will get stronger and stronger and stronger until you break it by accepting Christ as your personal Savior."

She continued to talk, but there seemed to be no response, except that Linda began to quiet measurably. When Kay finally stopped talking, Linda lay motionless, giving no response that she had even heard what the older girl had said. Reluctantly Kay rose to leave. Only then did Linda stir and take hold of her fingers with both her hands.

"Thank you, Kay," she whispered.

"If you would only trust Christ as your Savior, Linda, you would find things so different."

Their eyes met.

"I–I'll be thinking about it."

"You do that. Danny and I will be praying for you."

Kay switched out the light as she left, and Linda Penner was in the room alone.

For the space of a minute or two she sat on the bed, staring into the darkness. What Kay had said was true. She had made a mess of her life – a horrible mess. And there wasn't a thing she could do about it.

Or was there?

Her dad, the pastor, Danny and Kay, all told her the same thing. She was in trouble because Satan ruled her life. She was under his control. Numbly she got to her feet, turned on the light once more, and went over to the dresser where her Bible was lying.

Some verses she had memorized in Sunday school a long time ago began to come back to her. They were in the book of Romans somewhere in the ninth or tenth chapter. It was a moment before she found them.

> *If you confess with your mouth the Lord Jesus and believe in your heart that God has raised him from the dead, you will be saved. For with the heart one believes unto righteousness, and with the mouth confession is made unto salvation.*

The words seemed to leap out at her. They were more than words. They were flames burning into the very depths of her heart. *You will be saved. . . . You will be saved.*

It was so simple – so appealing. All she had to do was confess her sin and ask Jesus to take over in her heart.

But if she became a Christian, what then? She probably would never have any more fun. Linda lay down on the bed, her eyes wide and staring.

She was still lying there, her mind whirling, when the phone rang. A moment later Jim Morgan sang out.

"Hey, Linda! Jack Ross wants to talk to you."

For a brief instant Linda hesitated, almost as though she was about to drop to her knees. Then she got slowly to her feet, shrugging away her conviction. Jack Ross wanted to talk to her. Maybe the future wasn't going to be so bad after all.

The smile came back to her lips, and she swaggered defiantly as she went to take her phone call.

THE DANNY ORLIS SERIES

The Danny Orlis series, by Bernard Palmer, delivers a blend of adventure, mystery, and suspense through various settings—from the Canadian wilderness to Guatemalan jungles. Danny Orlis, an adept outdoorsman, skilled athlete, and committed Christian, employs his quick thinking, calm bravery, and biblical solutions to confront everyday problems and hair-raising dangers. Early stories focus on Danny navigating school life, sports, and outdoor challenges, while in later books, Danny and his wife Kay provide wisdom and guidance to youngsters facing lifelike situations and challenges. Having sold over two million copies, this series has made Palmer a renowned author in Christian youth literature. Palmer is also the author of the Felicia Cartright series and various other series for Christian youth.

AVAILABLE FROM WWW.ANEKOPRESS.COM

9 798889 360148